HOMICIDAL ALIENS
and Other Disappointments

HOMICIDAL ALIENS

and Other Disappointments

BRIAN YANSKY

CANDLEWICK PRESS

First edition 2013

Library of Congress Catalog Card Number 2013931461
ISBN 978-0-7636-5962-2

13 14 15 16 17 18 BVG 10 9 8 7 6 5 4 3 2 1

Printed in Berryville, VA, U.S.A.

This book was typeset in Mendoza.

Candlewick Press
99 Dover Street
Somerville, Massachusetts 02144

visit us at www.candlewick.com

For my parents, Bill and Agnes Yansky

PROLOGUE

So here's what happened, fellow earthlings, though I'm sure you already know: aliens landed, took over the world in ten seconds, killed millions of people, enslaved the survivors, and pretty much started colonizing like Earth belonged to them.

And the truth? I won't lie. It did. Pretty much.

THE END

Well, not *the* THE END. There's a Part Two.

These aliens, who call themselves Sanginians, like to say they are the greatest beings in the known universe. And yeah, they have awesome powers. They can conquer a world faster than we can brush our teeth or send a text. But here's one thing they didn't count on when they conquered Earth: We humans are stubborn about total annihilation of our species. And, as a general rule, we're reluctant to die. We aren't going to just hand our world over to them and say, "Take it. Hope you like it. Have a nice day." I don't want them to like it. I don't want them to have a nice day. I don't want them to ever have a nice day on this world. Have a terrible day, Sanginians.

My friends and I were enslaved like most of the survivors, but we didn't stay slaves. We found a way out. We escaped. We stole a Sanginian ship in Austin and traveled across West Texas to the steep mountains of northern New Mexico, where we'd heard there was a rebel camp. We met the rebels at the same time that an alien lord, *the* alien lord, their leader here on Earth, caught up with us in Taos. Sucked. Big-time.

The alien lord's name was Lord Vertenomous, and he'd come to collect his property (me, my friends)— what they like to call product. He was crazy powerful in the way the aliens are powerful: mind power, telepathic power. He was going to kill us, but the rebels attacked. Somehow, in the confusion of their attack, I killed Lord Vertenomous. He was saying, "I am sorry for your loss" left and right—which is what they say when they kill us because they are polite killers (you have to give them that)—when I turned him off. Fifteen rebels lay scattered on the ground, dead, and minds all around me were weeping with loss, but I killed the son of a female dog (my way of swearing due to a promise I made my now-dead mother) before he killed us all.

That was something. Not enough, but something.

How could I kill Lord Vertenomous when the aliens are so powerful? Extreme luck. And I'm changed. I'm not the same boy I was when the aliens invaded. It turns out I had their kind of telepathic/telekinetic power buried in my brain all along. Big surprise. Humongous. The same awakening happened to a lot of us survivors, maybe all, though my abilities are, well, extreme. And it isn't because I've got a big brain. Lauren, my sort-of girl-friend, is the smartest person I know, and she's one of the weakest as far as telepathic power. Go figure. I don't know why I'm strong, but I'll use this new strength and anything else I can to fight the aliens.

The rebels don't believe my "luck" explanation. Well, not most of them, anyway. I can feel some think it must be luck.

"You're damn right it's luck," says one guy about my age, blond hair, his mind as prickly as a porcupine.

But most of the rebels don't feel that way. I can hear them think things like *Warrior* and *New blood* and *At last!*

The rebels aren't like me or Lauren. They're like Catlin, my other friend who I escaped with. They're what the rebels call "talented"—people who had tele-pathic powers *before* the aliens invaded, like long before, like back in Roman times. The rebels say the talented are all over the world and are divided into twelve dif-ferent houses named for Roman gods: Jupiter, Neptune, Apollo, Venus, Mars, Diana, Minerva, Pluto, Vulcan, Juno, Mercury, and Saturn. According to Catlin, each house has different local clans, and there were many of these before the invasion, but now no one knows how many clans are left.

The rebels think my killing Lord Vert is the fulfill-ment of a myth that goes all the way back to the origins of the houses in Roman days. The myth of the Warrior Spirit.

According to this myth, the Warrior Spirit will come to one of its choosing in a time of great need, and it will fill him or her with a power great enough to save the talented. It's a prophecy as old as the talented themselves, like before Christ even. A lot of the rebels have been waiting and praying to their gods (yep, they have more than one) for the Chosen One to hurry up and get here. And many of them think he finally has.

"I'm sorry," I tell them. "Wrong dude." I'm not the Chosen One or the Chosen Anything. I feel lost most of the time. Afraid. Sad. Mad. Helpless. I wish I could be more than I am, but I'm just me.

But here's the thing about desperate people: they want to believe in something; they need to believe in something. So the rebels see me kill the leader of the aliens, and they think they've found their Warrior Spirit. And nothing I can say will convince them otherwise.

(((((1)))))

After I kill Lord Vertenomous, we load up the trucks, laying the bodies of the dead all together in one truck bed, then drive up a windy mountain road that ends, miles later, at a ski lodge parking lot. The rebels drive their trucks and cars and motorcycles right up to the edge of the thick pine forest, where we all hop out. A few rebels cover the vehicles with tree branches. Some others stay with the bodies. The rest of us follow a wide path into the pines and up the mountain from the lodge. In the lead is Doc, the old, white-haired guy who convinced the other rebels to let me, Lauren, and Catlin join their group. Following close on his heels is the blond guy about my age who didn't want to let us join the rebels. The sky is blue, the air fresh and clean. There's a sweet smell, sweet taste. I close my eyes and try to pretend I'm just a lucky camper taking a walk in the woods.

I start to hear some of my fellow rebels' random thoughts, which pretty much ruin the camper fantasy. The mundane and the terrible whisper all around me.

I wish I had an apple.

I miss my phone.

More dead. More always dead.

Why can't we drive closer to camp?

Need a bath.

That guy in front of me definitely needs a bath.

Dead. We'll all be dead soon.

I'm so afraid.

Then I hear a scream. I crouch and cover my ears. But it's not a real scream; it's a scream inside someone's mind, and it's being projected directly into *my* mind. I see what they see. I see the face of one of the dead, and I experience losing someone I love, through this other mind, again. I'm alone like they're alone — the way losing someone separates you so completely from everyone else — and I think of my parents and friends and all those I've lost, and I curse under my breath (sorry, Mom) that someone makes me feel that loss again.

I hear more voices, feel more pain as the news spreads. I try to shove that pain back on those who force it at me.

Then the voices do fade. I still hear them, but it's not like before. They're the low mumble of a distant crowd.

I see the path and woods again, feel the sprinkle of sun-light through the leaves.

Off to the right of us, wide paths are cut through the trees, creating slopes for skiers who no longer exist. Then the trees thicken, and I can't see them anymore. We walk for twenty minutes, the path getting steeper so that everyone is panting pretty hard by the time it levels into a slight slope. The woods thicken even more around us, and the patches of sunlight disappear entirely until we come around a bend and stop at a small clearing. Cliffs rise on two sides, and a gurgling stream slips effortlessly between them and rushes down the mountain. Off to the left is a meadow with blue flowers, which makes me think of the aliens and their plantings in Austin: trees with big blue leaves the size of dinner plates. These blue flowers aren't alien, though. They're ours, small with petals like daisies, fragile looking. If we were on vaca-tion, this would be an awesome spot. But we aren't on vacation. We will never be on vacation.

Sometimes a thought like this sets off an avalanche of never-bes. Never be with my family again. Never be in my home. Never be in college. Never be, never be. The never-bes can fill you with all that isn't and can't be if you're not careful. And maybe even if you are.

We enter the camp on the side where the supply cave is. The rebels have raided a lot of stores in Santa Fe and Taos, and they've got camping equipment and all kinds of things in the supply cave. Lauren, Catlin, and I are all given tents and sleeping bags and some other basics and told to set up camp in Section 4. Lots of tents dot the wooded hillside. We walk past Sections 1, 2, and 3, numbers marked on tree trunks, out to the less crowded Section 4.

As we pass through camp, I'm shocked and pleased to see children and old people among the rebels. Back in Austin there were almost no grandparents or even parents and no little sisters or brothers. We thought they had all been murdered by the aliens.

My hand moves into the pocket of my jeans and feels for the paper calendar there. It was given to me by one of those few older people imprisoned by Lord Vert. Her name was Betty. She kept track of the days since the invasion because she was determined not to let the aliens take time from us even as they took everything else. She gave me the calendar right before she killed herself. I'm the keeper of days now, and I keep them for Betty and myself and because it's one small thing the aliens haven't been able to take. Every small thing we keep matters.

I hear people thinking my name everywhere we walk, which is kind of creepy. And, yeah, maybe a tiny bit cool, too—for about a second. *Jesse, his name is Jesse. He killed an alien lord. They say the spirit fills him.*

"They say." My mother, the English teacher, hated

when someone said "They say." She wasn't one to let linguistic imprecision pass. "They who?" she would ask, raising her eyebrows. If the president of the United States had said, "They say," she would have stopped him cold with her raised eyebrows and said, "And just who is 'they,' Mr. President?" He would have answered, too. Nobody ignored my mom. Nobody.

"They" are wrong, I mindspeak. *No spirit fills me. I never even had school spirit.*

For a second, unexpectedly, I miss my high school. Not just my friends, who I've missed a thousand times since the invasion, but the actual building where I was forced to sit through boring lectures and take tests and eat food that was not always clearly identifiable.

We set up camp on a flat section just below a rocky ledge, a spot that Lauren picks for its privacy and levelness. I can see Catlin approves, but I'd rather be farther off, up the hill. Using her class president voice, Lauren directs us to set up our tents in a little triangle around a space where we dig a pit for a fire. We are about to head out to gather firewood when one of our neighbors—a tall, thin woman with a British accent—tells us we can't light fires because of the alien patrol ships.

"Great," I say. "That's just double frickin' great."

Everyone, including me, is a little surprised by the anger in my voice.

"I just wanted to roast marshmallows," I say, which, I know, sounds completely ridiculous.

Some part of me, the ridiculous part I guess, thought reaching the rebel camp meant reaching freedom. But the aliens are still here. They're still everywhere. I'm not free.

I feel Catlin understand, hear her understand, and for a second I think she's going to touch me on the shoulder, but she doesn't. Lauren just looks irritated. I don't blame her. I'm being ungrateful. Weak. Still, I'm irritated by her irritation. She reminds me of my mother when she was giving me a failing grade over some behavior. I quickly bury this thought. I'm not the smartest guy when it comes to girls, but I'm smart enough to know that getting caught comparing your girlfriend to your mother is a poor relationship move.

A bell calls us to dinner. We follow a path over to the eating area. Three women and a man ladle stew into plastic bowls, which they serve with two pieces of bread. The rebels eat at picnic tables that circle a small clearing. The tables are painted an earthy brown and are mostly back in the trees, though I worry that some of them, if the aliens fly low enough, could be seen from the air. There are probably two hundred people eating, maybe more. Some white, some Hispanic, some Native American, a few African-American, a few Asian. Rainbow crowd.

And there are little kids being little kids. Complaining. Arguing. Playing. There's a crying baby. A baby! I shouldn't be all that happy to hear the less-than-sweet sound of a crying infant, but I am. I am.

A little blond girl from the next table shyly looks my way and mindspeaks, *Are you here to save us?*

I should tell the truth. After all we've all been through, we deserve the truth. But she's so little, and the truth is so cruel: *I can't save anyone. I don't know why I'm here.* I don't say it.

Instead I mindspeak, *Eat your vegetables.*

She gives me a deserved look of contempt.

"Sorry," I say.

"For what?" Lauren says.

Catlin knows, but Lauren can't hear what's in other minds very well and misses most of what's gone on between the little girl and me. It's like she's deaf almost. I should tell her, but I'm hungry and tired and I just don't feel like it. I tell her the last part about telling the little girl to eat her vegetables.

"You'll make a good father," she says.

Which just about causes me to spit my stew out. Even before the end of the world, I wasn't ready to start thinking of myself as a father, and now . . . now I can't imagine it. I can't imagine anyone having children in this world.

· · • ● • · ·

After dinner, Doc invites us to a meeting. I'm so tired, I feel like I could sleep sitting up at the table, so I sure don't want to go to a meeting. But most people are getting up and dutifully heading in the direction Doc pointed us toward.

Lauren and Catlin stand up, and I'm about to give in when I start to choke. It doesn't feel like that. It feels like hands are around my throat, squeezing. Fingers digging in. I fight for breath but stagger helplessly. Then I'm falling. I see Lord Vertenomous. It's like I've traveled back to the plaza in Taos. The brick walkway beneath me; low, crowded stucco buildings all around; the pale-blue sky gone milky. Just like then.

None of this makes any sense, but it seems so real. I hear what I heard back then. The sounds of people dying: calling to each other, screaming, crying, falling.

Then somehow I'm standing up, and I'm in that moment when I found a way to kill Lord Vertenomous and he fell, dead. But now I'm fighting another alien, too — not Lord Vertenomous, not nearly as strong as he was, but an alien all the same and in the same square — and I'm losing. More people are dying.

What is happening to me?

Then, just as quickly, I'm right back on the bench, and Lauren and Catlin are looking at me with concern. I realize then that I've been on the bench this whole time while also in that other place. I'm shaky. I grip the table, as if holding tight can keep me from slipping away.

"Are you all right?" Lauren says.

"Not really," I say, but then try to smile. "Fine. I'm fine. Must be the rich food."

What just happened? Flashback? Some kind of message? Could I have somehow fallen asleep and dreamed? Nothing makes sense so I choose what my mom would have called a typical male reaction: I try to pretend it didn't really happen.

Catlin, Lauren, and I walk down one of the narrow paths near the supply caves. I realize that I actually like the way the woods feel. I'm a city boy, but these woods, foreign to me before the aliens came, feel less foreign now. And the cities feel more foreign. Like graveyards, empty and haunted.

I notice something as we walk. A faint hum in the trees and bushes. I feel my muscles tense.

"Do you hear that?" I whisper.

Lauren listens and looks at me with something close to that little girl's look when I told her to eat her vegetables. "Bugs?"

"Oh, right," I say. But then I realize that bugs mean more than just bugs. Bugs mean everything didn't die when the aliens conquered us. Score one for the home planet. We have bugs.

"I saw a squirrel earlier," Catlin says. "I asked

someone if I'd really seen what I thought I'd seen, and they said there were some animals out here. I guess the aliens focused their killing ray on the cities. The damage doesn't seem as complete here."

"Killing ray?" I say, raising my eyebrow in a Spockian way. Or trying anyway. No one could raise a single eyebrow like Spock.

"What would you call it?"

Both Catlin and I like retro science-fiction movies. We've talked about them before. We like the good ones or the ones that are so bad they're good. I quote from one that falls in the latter category: "Death ray."

She thinks about it and smiles. *"Teenagers from Outer Space."*

"Exactly," I say. "A classically bad, really bad, movie."

I see a scene from the movie in her mind. It's when a dog gets zapped into a skeleton by a ray gun. This telepathic power we have is totally weird, but on the plus side, we get to share a truly awful scene from *Teenagers from Outer Space.*

"You shouldn't joke about it," Lauren says, glaring at Catlin, though she manages to save enough of the feeling to give me a quick look of disapproval.

She walks faster so she gets ahead of us. I'm surprised by her reaction. She must know we aren't joking because we think it's funny ha-ha. We're joking because it's too terrible not to joke. But then I feel bad, like I've laughed at a funeral or something.

"I'm sorry," Catlin says to Lauren.

I apologize, too, but the whole thing makes me realize that Lauren and I don't really know each other all that well. I mean, we have a connection and all. From back at Lord Vertenomous's. And we kissed once in that abandoned grocery store in West Texas when we were traveling here. But things seem different now. Maybe I just need to try harder to understand the way she sees things.

The light is dim, almost gone. Our campsite is only a few hundred yards up from the clearing where the meeting is, but I still worry about finding it in the dark. Funny how a big, horrible worry doesn't wipe out all the little worries. They're like bugs. They survive no matter what.

(((((2)))))

Bluish lights spread around the edge of the clearing, creating a glow that resembles moonlight. It's just enough to guide me and Lauren and Catlin through the clearing without bumping into anything or anyone. Even in the dim light, I can see that a lot of people are already here. I can feel them, too, even more clearly than I can see them. They feel confused. And suspicious. And hopeful. And scared. Some of these thoughts come from the same people, one right after another like machine-gun fire. Being telepathic doesn't exactly clear up the human psyche. In fact, there's a lot of confusion and contradiction in most people, which is both comforting (at least I'm not the only one) and disturbing (we're totally messed up).

Now that the sun's down, the temperature is falling fast. A fire would be nice. A fire should be our right as human beings. Even cavemen and cavewomen sat around fires and discussed caveman and cavewoman things, like maybe the best size for a club or whether a leopard skin was better than a bear skin on cold winter nights. But here we are back in the forest, this time the hunted and not the hunters, without even a fire to keep us warm.

I hate them, I think. *I hate them so much.*

"Ouch," Catlin says. "Careful."

Others are looking at me.

"Your anger," she says. "It's like you pinched me."

"You felt that?"

"I didn't feel anything," Lauren says, her earlier disapproval sneaking back into her voice. "Or not much, anyway."

"You don't realize how strong you are," Catlin says. "You have to control your feelings, or block them from us at least."

"Sorry," I say to those sitting closest to me.

"Don't worry about it," one of them says. "You'll learn."

"It was a whisper," Lauren says stubbornly, "if it was anything."

This is hard for Lauren. She is used to being the smartest person in a room. She was going to be valedictorian at her school. But this telepathic kind of mind power is different from intelligence. If Albert Einstein showed up, he'd still be the smartest person alive, but he might be a telepathic moron. He'd be all, "But I discovered the theory of relativity. Ever heard of $E = mc^2$?" Wouldn't matter. That would be hard on Einstein. It's hard on Lauren.

More people come into the clearing, including Doc and another old guy whose long white hair is tied back in a ponytail and who makes about two Docs in size. They stand on a raised platform backed up against a row of trees. The crowd gathers in front of them, filling up rows of split-log benches that form a semicircle around the platform.

Doc is small and neat, with white hair and one of those pointy white beards, like Colonel Sanders had. His real name is Lorenzo Sergio de Cabeza, so it's not hard to understand why I'm relieved he goes by Doc. He looks like a professor, which makes sense since he was one; his nickname comes from his two PhDs.

"First, I'd like to welcome the newest members of our group to our town meeting," Doc says. "Could the new members please come to the front?"

Lauren, the great joiner, smiles enthusiastically and leads us toward the stage. Catlin has the same pained expression I imagine on my face, but we obediently follow. Two others—a young boy and an older girl who's about our age—step forward from Doc's right.

As I follow Lauren up front, a buzz of inner voices says things like *New bloods* and *Not of the House of Jupiter and Clan of Wind* and *Jesse* and *The Warrior Spirit*. At least I hear a few dissenting voices. Someone thinks, *That can't be the one with the Warrior Spirit in him. No heroic glow.*

The new boy and girl look like they might be siblings. They're both tall and thin, with huge blue eyes and short, uneven blond hair.

Doc says that before we begin we should have a moment of silence for the dead. "There'll be a funeral service tomorrow at dawn," Doc adds. "In the graveyard." And then the silence. It's the noisiest silence I've ever experienced. I hear everyone. I feel what others are feeling, too. It hurts. Losing someone hurts so much. I can't breathe. I can't think. I feel like I'm drowning, like there's no way I'll get back to the surface. It wasn't this way back at Lord Vertenomous's. It was never this strong, never so everywhere at once. More pain comes at me. It's like being stung all over by bees.

Doc touches me on the back, and the voices drop away to a whisper. I think he's done something, and I feel relief and gratitude. I take deep breaths.

You have to shield yourself, or the voices will overwhelm you. They think they're shielded, but they aren't. Not from you. So you're going to have to shield yourself. Watch me, and try to do what I do.

He shows me how to shield. It's sort of like pulling a curtain, an invisible one, around myself, then thickening it to keep out the sounds. It takes me a few tries, and even then my shield's not nearly as strong as his, but it's a definite improvement.

Good, he thinks. *It will keep your thoughts hidden, too. You can control what you show and what is shown to you. You see?*

"I think so," I say.

As Doc returns to the platform, I turn to Lauren to see if I can help her block out the voices, but she doesn't seem bothered by them.

Doc introduces us to the crowd—the boy and girl are named Zack and Zelda—and says we make fifty-two newcomers. He says it's time we stopped thinking of ourselves as Wind Clan or Thunder Clan of the House of Jupiter or the House of Apollo and started thinking of ourselves as New America.

"It's a new world," he says, "and we are the survivors. It's time we became something new and inclusive. We'll be like America once was to the rest of the world. We will welcome all. New America. What say others?"

Others say a lot—though most of them don't use their mouths. Some think New Bloods (those of us who changed because of contact with the aliens) and people from other houses can't be trusted, shouldn't be trusted.

Some agree with Doc, though, and think all survivors should unite.

Someone mindspeaks, *If the Spirit of the Warrior comes to one from outside the houses and clans, all has changed. We must change.*

If, someone else mindspeaks doubtfully. *If.*

The man beside Doc, the one who makes two of him, raises his massive arms. He has brown, leathery skin and a wide, blunt nose. The voices go silent.

"I'm Running Bird, for those of you who don't know me," he says, looking right at me.

My first thought is *Don't you mean Flying Bird?* But then I remember there is a bird that runs: the roadrunner. Then I hear something strange even in this strange new world. I hear *"Beep beep!"* in my mind — the sound of the roadrunner from the cartoon.

"Also called Sam White. I'm a real, live Navajo, Hispanic, white, African-American American, in case you're wondering. All of you better put aside all your prejudices against New Bloods and other houses and Native American, Hispanic, white, African-American Americans because the aliens are coming for us. I saw in a dream that the House of Vulcan is no more. I saw it, and it is true. If we are to survive, we have to join together."

Voices in the crowd are saying that the House of Vulcan is strong and cannot be destroyed, but we all know it can. We have been conquered. The conquered know things that the unconquered don't. One of the things the conquered know is that anything can be destroyed.

"Alien hunters track us," Running Bird says. "Doc is right. We need every survivor we can get. We are all New America or we are lost."

"We are the Clan of the Wind of the House of Jupiter," someone says, and I see that someone is the blond guy again. "We are two thousand years old, and we will survive. Running Bird's vision just makes it clearer how. We must hide. I will lead us to the caves in Mexico my grandfather showed me. I will lead the way."

Dylan. I hear his name in the minds of others. And something else: *Doc's son.* I see the physical resemblance, though Dylan is lighter in color than Doc and muscular and has long, straight blond hair. But I had a strong feeling of trust when I met Doc, and I feel just as strongly about Dylan — only the feeling is the opposite.

Running Bird says, "The aliens will track us wherever we go. We cannot hide."

"The caves will protect us," says Dylan. "No one knows about them but me. We can survive in the caves."

Running Bird shakes his head. "And then what?"

"We will build a city below the earth, and we will grow stronger. We will live. And someday we'll return to the surface. Someday it will be safe. But until that day, we will live under the ground. And in the future they'll tell stories about us and how we saved mankind."

Stories about him. He thinks they'll tell stories about *him*. I feel his yearning for these stories.

There are a lot of voices then. Most of them agree with Dylan. *Run. Hide. Live.* I get it. I understand. *Run, hide, live* sounds better than *stay, fight, die.* If those are the choices, then I'm with the majority. Are those the choices?

If I remember right, the humans in the Matrix movies hide in caves to escape the machines, but their city is annihilated and they are nearly wiped out. That's an ending I want to avoid. Okay, it's just a movie, but hiding seems wrong to me.

My friends and I thought the aliens were too strong and we had no choice but to be slaves in order to survive. But then Betty walked up to one of the aliens and slapped him. *Crack!* Right across the face. A beautiful sound. He killed her, but for a second she blocked him — actually blocked him. And that's when we knew: the aliens aren't invincible. Awesomely powerful, yes. Invincible, no. It's the kind of difference that makes fighting possible.

They're not too strong to fight.

At first I think someone else says this, but then I realize it's me. Mindspeak. It just slips out. A couple hundred eyes turn toward me. I probably have that deer-caught-in-headlights look, but I know I have to say something.

"My friends and I fought them. We escaped from them. They're not all-powerful. They can be defeated." I try to hide my doubt. I don't think I'm all that successful.

But I know more. A secret. Something that a friendly Sanginian—there is such a thing, if you can believe that—told me and Catlin and Lauren. Something that not even Running Bird or Doc could know. More aliens are coming. Settlers out there in ships are on their way to Earth right now. And if we're huddled in caves waiting to get strong enough to fight aliens, we'll most likely never be strong enough because they will fill the planet. I almost say this. Almost. But I stop myself because it feels overwhelming, like telling this crowd about the aliens will be like telling them to give up. Might as well hide in caves and live out the rest of our miserable lives and give up Earth. I can't accept that. I won't.

"This meeting isn't about staying or running," Doc says. He lets his eyes rest on Dylan a second before going on. "There will be time for that. This meeting is about understanding we're a new country, all of us. We are New America."

"Every meeting is about staying or running," Dylan says.

Father and son glare at each other, the resemblance clearer than ever. Then an image appears in my mind. It's Dylan and his father in a tent lit by a lamp. Dylan is looking down at his father, who's on a cot or something.

And Dylan is trying to look sad, but he doesn't *feel* sad. He feels almost . . . happy. He does feel happy.

The image disappears but leaves me feeling confused and a little freaked. It's like that vision of me fighting the alien in Taos. It feels like more than just my admittedly overactive imagination. It feels real. But it can't be. I'm so tired. I need to sleep. Maybe I just need sleep.

"We will vote on the creation of New America," Doc says, ignoring his son.

Some people want more discussion, though, and so they go around and around again for another fifteen or twenty minutes.

At last they vote. New America wins by a narrow majority. I wonder if it was this way when old America, those struggling colonies, decided they were a country. Here in the rebel camp, people celebrate. A few people slap me and Lauren and Catlin on the back, welcoming us into New America. The truth is, I don't feel so much happy as relieved. We don't have to leave.

I'm about to head back to camp with Lauren, Catlin, and the other newbies, Zack and Zelda. But before I manage to work my way out of the crowd, Doc summons me with mindspeak. Now what?

"You guys go on," I say to my friends.

Catlin looks at me funny, like she's worried about me. For just a second I wonder if she saw what I saw, the daydream or whatever it was of Doc and Dylan. But I know she didn't. Lauren just shrugs, says, "See you back at camp," and leads Zelda and Zack back down the trail. Catlin is the last to go.

I head back over to the platform, where Doc, Running Bird, and another man are waiting for me.

It turns out my shield wasn't quite as effective as I'd hoped, because Doc heard me thinking about what the Sanginian smuggler told us back in Austin.

"How many settlers?" Doc asks.

I don't bother pretending I'm confused by the question. "He said thirty million would be here soon."

"Thirty million," Running Bird says like he's cursing.

"Then all is lost," the third man says. He's fair skinned, but he gets even paler. "We can't fight thirty million."

"He told me—the smuggler," I say when I see their questioning expressions. "This alien smuggler. He said it wasn't, you know, inevitable. The aliens might not settle here if they had a reason not to."

There isn't any big sigh of relief over this minute possibility from Doc, Running Bird, or the third man. No one says, "Well, that changes things, doesn't it?" The third man, who Doc introduces as Robert Penderson, says, "I don't understand. They're already here. What would keep more from coming?"

"I don't know," I admit.

"The Chosen One is right," Running Bird says. "We

cannot fight thirty million, but maybe we can fight however many thousands are here and keep the thirty million from coming. Maybe we can do that. The spirit in the boy speaks from the depths of the prophecy."

Depths of the prophecy? Does anyone ever say stuff like that? Running Bird does, I guess.

"It came from the mouth of an alien, not from the depths of any prophecy," I say.

"But it isn't the alien who delivers this message to us. It is you," Running Bird insists.

"Catlin or Lauren could have told you the same thing," I point out.

"But *you* told us."

"Because Doc called me back."

"It is written, and what is written will be."

"What's that even mean? Written where? By who?" I know I sound angry and confused, but that's because I'm, well, angry and confused.

"It means everything is written down in the Big Book. All that has happened, is happening, and will happen is already written."

"In the Big Book," I say. "What big book?"

"*The* Big Book."

"That clears things up. Thanks."

"We have existed, exist, will exist. It's just an illusion that moments come and go, that there is a past separate from the present separate from the future. That people are born, then live, then die. All of that is going on all the time—past, present, and future. We just can't see it. Clearer?"

Doc and Robert Penderson look like this is not the first time they've heard Running Bird talk like this, but that they wish maybe it was. I wonder what my mother would have said to him. I wish she were here. I wish that a lot.

"Why don't you just take a look in the Big Book, then?" I say. "You'll see I'm not this Chosen One."

"Doesn't work that way. Only the Creator can look at the Big Book. We mortals sometimes, if we're very, very lucky, get glimpses. Even other gods, like the Warrior, don't get much of a look. The Creator is stingy that way."

"Wait," I say, trying to smile dismissively. "Are you saying you think I might be infected with the spirit of a *god*?"

"Not infected," Running Bird says, sounding offended. "Blessed."

I'm saved from having to discuss my infection/ blessing further by Robert Penderson, who starts muttering, "Thirty million. Thirty million coming."

"We'll find a way, Robert," Doc says, placing a hand on the guy's shoulder.

"Meanwhile," Doc says to me, "keep this to yourself,

Jesse. People are already panicked enough. We don't want to make them worse."

"Lauren and Catlin know," I remind him.

"Tell them to tell no one."

As I walk up toward our campsite through the thick, dark woods, I think, *All of it is right here and right now— the past, the present, and the future.* All of it? How can that be? My mother would give a clear grammatical explanation for why this shouldn't be allowed. Verbs tell time. End of story. Time can't just ignore grammar. I smile thinking this because I can hear my mother's voice.

Whatever that Big Book of Running Bird's says, I feel one thing. I'm tired of running. I want to fight. No matter what, I want to fight.

3

When I get to the campsite, Lauren, Catlin, Zack, and Zelda are sitting around where our fire would be if we could have a fire. Which we can't.

The cold seeps through my thin jacket. A fire would make the whole night better. A flickering orange in the dark to light up our faces, a source of heat to warm our hands. Is it too much to ask?

I'm pretty sure heroes don't whine. They quietly endure cold, fireless nights. Further proof I'm no hero.

Someone coughs from one of the tents, and from not far off in the woods, something scurries over leaves. A small animal? I trip over a root as I try to sit next to Lauren. I land harder than planned next to her. She puts her arm around me, which lightens my darkening mood. Lauren doesn't expect me to be a hero. She knows that if we have any chance of defeating the aliens, we'll do it by working together, not because of the mysterious powers of some prophesized Chosen One.

Lauren asks me what I needed to talk to Doc about, and, because of the presence of Zack and Zelda, I say that I just wanted to learn a little more about the camp. Lame, I know.

"So what did you find out?" Lauren says.

"That that Running Bird/Sam White guy is one weird dude."

"He was a priest of the House of Jupiter," Catlin says. "My mother met him once. I remember her talking about him, how powerful he was. But he broke his vows after his wife died—killed by a drunk driver or something. He was pretty young, I think."

"He's a priest of Weirdness now," I say.

Then, before someone asks me to explain, I ask Zelda and Zack about how they got here. They say they walked all the way from Denver.

"We were lucky to get away," Zelda says. "A lot of people didn't. Our parents and our aunt and uncle and cousins didn't. We had some close calls getting here. Then I heard the whisper of minds in these mountains. We found the camp."

"You have that talent?" Catlin says.

"What talent?" Lauren asks.

"Some people can hear farther than most," Catlin says. "Not many. It's a very powerful talent."

"I'm lucky," Zelda says, her face flushing a little. I can feel it flush, feel the heat in her body rise, even though I can't see her clearly.

"Did everyone in your clan have this talent?" Lauren asks. I can hear her wanting to catalog and organize information. I can hear her curiosity and the reach of her mind. She always impresses me.

Zelda says her clan members could predict the weather, tell if someone was lying, sometimes make people see things that weren't there for a second or two, and sometimes see what someone might do or had done. Also, many were good fighters. A lot of them worked in law enforcement or in the military.

"So houses tend to have certain talents?" I say.

Catlin answers that they do. Her house, the House of Venus, is known to be good at affecting people's emotions. They can calm people or anger them. Many of them were good healers—nurses and doctors and psychiatrists.

I turn to the shadowy figure of Zack, thinking maybe I'll ask him what his abilities are since he seems too shy to join the conversation on his own. But even in the dark, I can tell that Zack is looking right at me—and that he probably has been for quite some time.

"Is something wrong?" I ask him.

"It's just . . . you don't sound like I thought he'd sound. The Chosen One, I mean."

His voice breaks in that unlucky way a voice does sometimes when a totally normal boy is asking something important. The whole miserable "suddenly a girl has inhabited your vocal cords" experience. Luckily, I'm past that phase. Well, like, 98 percent past it, anyway.

The girls giggle.

Showing male solidarity, I turn away from the girls. "That's because I'm not him," I say.

"You don't really look like the Chosen One," Zelda says.

"He doesn't?" Catlin sounds surprised. An irritating flush burns my cheeks. Maybe the lack of a fire isn't such a bad thing after all.

"I mean like I imagined him. You know. Big. Ripped like a superhero or like Thor or something."

"The Chosen One isn't that way," Catlin says. "It's his mind that's strong, and his spirit. He's caring, and he fights for everyone. The spirit of the Warrior chooses him because he has qualities that make him a good leader."

They all look at me. I'm totally behind the no-fire rule now.

"Oh, come on," Lauren says, using her A-student voice. "We all know there's no such thing as the Warrior Spirit or the Chosen One. It's a story—a myth invented to give people hope during really hard times."

She looks around like she expects a chorus of

agreement, but she doesn't get one. Even I feel oddly reluctant to side with her, despite agreeing with everything she just said. What's holding me back? Crazy as it sounds, there have been times when I don't feel like myself. Like at the meeting, when I saw Doc and Dylan in some other place.

"They say you fight like the aliens," Zack says.

"He totally did," Catlin says. "He killed Lord Vertenomous."

"A lot of people were attacking him. It wasn't just me," I say.

"But *you* killed him," she says. "Maybe the spirit was in you then. Maybe it comes and goes."

"There was no spirit," I say. "It was just me."

I killed him. Me. Where there could — or maybe even should — be pride, there's shame. Alien lord. Mass murderer. Destroyer of the human race. Enslaver. Rapist. Lord Vertenomous was all those things, but it still feels wrong to kill. I had to do it. I know that. Maybe it's like what a soldier feels in war. Doing things you have to do can still make you feel empty inside. I shove the feeling away, and it goes, but not willingly and not as far as I'd like.

"I wish I could be like you," Zack says to me. I can't really see him, but I can feel him, feel the yearning in him. "I wish I could kill one of them. I wish I could kill them all."

I want to tell him he doesn't, not really, but I don't say anything. We all stare at our fire that isn't there. There's the sound of someone unzipping a tent down from us. Other than that, it's a big silence.

Zack breaks it. "I don't have my talent yet, but I will. My father and uncle were both good fighters. That's what my talent will be. I'll be a fighter, and I will kill them."

"We saw a lot of people die," Zelda says, apologizing. She doesn't need to. I understand. We all understand.

"I don't care what happens to me," Zack says. "I just want to kill some of them."

"You have to care," Catlin says. "If we stop caring, we're lost."

"I care." His hands are balled fists; his body is stiff. "I care about killing them."

The aliens have taken everything from us. What did they leave behind? An empty space. What can fill an empty space? Hate. I didn't know that before, but I do now. If you're not careful, you can end up being all hate.

I grew up the son of a soldier, one who'd been to war, one who'd worked his way up to colonel. I heard stories about people who filled the emptiness with hate. They'd had their country taken away from them, had their families killed, had their homes destroyed. He said some of those people were capable of anything. They'd strap a bomb to themselves and explode it in a public place because hate was all they had.

"You can't stop caring, Zack, because we're all that's left," Zelda says. "There has to be more to us than just revenge. We have to be more. We're the ones who will make the new world when we defeat the aliens."

I feel like laughing at this—in an "Are you crazy?" kind of way. Defeat the aliens?

"As long as we fight," Zack says, the tightness in his voice easing a little.

"We'll fight," I say, placing a hand on Zack's shoulder and pretending confidence. But the truth? I struggle every moment just to have faith we'll survive another day.

After a while, exhausted, we all crawl into our tents. I don't even sneak over to Lauren's tent. I want to. I just can't keep my eyes open long enough to get up out of my sleeping bag once I've crawled into it. My eyes are so heavy. Everything is so heavy.

4

I dream of aliens. I see a fleet of ships. I'm seeing them from a long distance but not through a telescope. Sweet Son of God, I'm floating in space. The strange thing is, it's kind of cool. I can breathe fine. I'm big, too — as big as the moon.

Even with my enormous eyes, I can't see the end of the fleet. How can there be that many ships in the universe? But there are. Then, suddenly, in the way of dreams, I'm sucked out of space and into a room. I know immediately where I am. I'm in Lord Vertenomous's house. I begin to sweat. This is where I was a slave, lost friends, was almost murdered. There is no fight-or-flight discussion going on in my mind. My thoughts are all in agreement: *run.*

But I can't run. I can't even move. I can feel the fear coming out of me like sweat. I feel his presence. How is that possible? I killed him. How could he possibly be here? But then I realize that what I'm feeling is an alien's strength, his power, which is like Lord Vertenomous's but different somehow. Then I feel other aliens, many of them, in the house. It's like falling into a pit of snakes.

I keep thinking this isn't possible. Dream. I can't be back here. Dream. But I *can* be back here because my dreams aren't like other people's anymore. I can dream-walk. I can go places in my dreams. Never this far before, but here I am. I really, really wish I wasn't.

I finally am able to force myself to move. Do I do what I should and take off out the door like I'm being chased by bears or bulls? I do not. I move to the door. I can feel *him* just beyond it, hear his power like thunder crackling in the sky. Something is pulling me toward him. I go from being unable to move to being unable *not* to move. I remember being caught in one of those fast-moving Colorado streams once, the impossibly strong current banging me into rocks. I had no control then, just like I have no control now.

I open the door and look in and see an alien standing in front of one of their communication devices. He is small, with the greenish tint to his skin that all of them have and big round eyes. I also see his power, which radiates around him, a dark green with tiny explosions of blue. It's so intense, it blinds me for a second, and then it fades into him.

I don't know how an alien communication device works, but I know that it amplifies and directs their thoughts so they can communicate over vast distances, out in space even. I hear this alien reporting on finding and killing forty more humans. I think of Running Bird saying the House of Vulcan is destroyed and wonder if these are the forty.

The alien stops talking and turns. He's tense and aware, and he looks right at me. But the alien's eyes keep moving. They look all around the room. It's like a scan, his power reaching out, feeling for my presence. It breaks over me like a wave breaking onshore. It practically knocks me off my feet.

Who's there?

I feel zero desire to tell him. Well, that's not entirely true. I'd like to say, "Your worst nightmare" or something along those lines. I consider it, even, but then I decide I'd prefer to survive in silence than to have my one satisfying moment.

Here but not here, he thinks. He's puzzled. I can feel that. *Dreamwalker? On this planet? Extraordinary. I've never actually met one, but that's what you are, aren't you?*

He seems pleased. I know he can't see me, because he's not looking at me, but he's still scanning for me with his mind as he talks; he's listening, and I think he'll hear even the faintest sound. If a breath escapes my mouth, he'll find me. The air itself will creak.

You are one of them, aren't you, Prey? The product that is not product. And here you are, a dreamwalker. This is a surprise, and I do love surprises. Welcome, dreamwalker, I am your deathgiver. We all have to have a deathgiver sooner or later. Sooner in your case. Think of it this way: Most of us never have the opportunity to meet our deathgiver. You do. Happy deathday to you.

Great, I finally meet an alien with a sense of humor, and the big joke is that he's going to kill me. Good one. I should stay quiet, but I can't. *We celebrate birthdays, not deathdays, you freak of freaks.* (While all the aliens are freaks to us, I have the feeling that this one is even freakier than most.) *And I'm not product. You know I'm not. A lot of us aren't.*

Product was what they called us humans they didn't kill. In the beginning we were valuable because the Sanginians could link to us and manipulate us. We were special. Then we were *too* special. We were evolving, learning how to send messages and not just receive them. We became evidence then, evidence that they shouldn't have settled our planet because we weren't mindless, soulless animals. We became dangerous to the company. The alien company bringing the settlers has kept the existence of those of us who can "hear" a secret. They have no intention of losing their profit because a few humans aren't product.

Indeed not. Product certainly can't dreamwalk. This

means I will have to kill you even more quickly. Can't have you causing trouble for my employers, now, can I? And I have yet to meet anyone who causes trouble from the grave.

He pauses, and I can see that this is the part he likes the best: toying with his prey before he kills it. Cat and mouse. *I often tell my prey to come back from death and say hello. Some swear they will haunt me until I die. But do they? Never so much as a word. It's a disappointment, frankly. I fear there is no life after this one.* He sighs. *Oh, well. Live while you can, right?*

As he's talking, I step farther into the room. My words have probably given him my position or at least narrowed down where he thinks I am. That's reason enough to move, and I do — to the far wall. He finishes his little speech and then does something that pulls the air just to the right of me. It's almost like it's sucked away, like water pulled down a drain. It tries to pull me in, but I'm far enough away that I can move beyond it.

You're going to kill us for money, I think with as much contempt as I can. At the same time I duck and roll (thank you, nine years of martial arts) because he turns to where I am.

He thinks, *It sounds so petty when you say it that way. Money, I find, is a necessary evil. In the old days, a hunter was so valued he needed no money. Monarchs gave him palaces and females and warriors to fight for him and anything he desired. But these modern times require money. I* feel cheapened by it, but what can you do? Times change. Hunt and kill stay the same, though. Thank the One for that. I am what I do. It's a beautiful thing.

He strikes again. A different strike? This time it feels like a rip in the air, like something I could fall through. I'm pretty sure I wouldn't like where I ended up.

I'm coming for you, he thinks. *Don't disappoint me with weak tricks. Fight me, here and now. What's the use of running, anyway? Your time, your species' time, has passed. I have to say you haven't done a very good job keeping this planet up, either. It needs — what is the term? — a makeover. This world won't miss humans. So, time to go. There is no way out, dreamwalker. I'm sorry for your loss.*

I know he's trying to get me to say something. The fear is still pouring out of me, and I'm pretty sure he'll feel it or smell it or something. I do want to say something, a lot of somethings. I shouldn't. But —

Intercourse you, I think.

As I tuck and roll, I try to wake myself up. I say the word *wake* again and again, as if repeating it might spark a "There's no place like home" magic. At least I have the tiny victory of confusing the alien. *Intercourse me?* he thinks. *What does this mean?*

Wake. Wake. Wake. And then, finally, thankfully, I do. I'm back in my sleeping bag. I fight to catch my breath. I'm still sweating fear. It does not smell good. I'm pretty sure Eau de Fear will not be the scent of the future, or maybe it will if the aliens get their way. Deathday. It was so real. Deathgiver. He was so real.

Lying there in my warm bag, the cold all around me, I try to convince myself that it was just a dream. I don't have much luck. In the old world, there would have been no question. A dream was just a dream. But this isn't the old world.

I unzip my bag and dress quickly. The cold from the night feels sharp against my body and raises goose bumps on my arms. I think about waking Lauren, but it's early, the sun not even up above the mountain peaks to the west. I decide to go for a walk and then wake her. Only a few people in camp are awake and stomping around, shaking the cold from their sleepy bodies. I walk away from them and the camp.

The woods are dense with tall trees and undergrowth, but after a few minutes, I find a narrow trail. The sun rises over the mountain, and sunlight slides between leafy tree limbs. I walk for maybe another ten minutes before I come up against a massive cliff. It's so high that even leaning back as far as I can, I can't see the top. I could go around it, though it would take a long time. Or I could just head back to camp. I study the cliff for a minute and decide I can climb it. This is a stupid decision—it isn't like I don't have enough excitement in my life—but that doesn't dissuade me. Somehow stupid is appealing at the moment.

And so I climb up the too-steep and too-crumbly cliff, losing my footing a couple of times and nearly falling to what would most likely be my death. On the bright side, that would make my deathgiver this cliff and not some smug alien hunter. Not all that bright when I actually think it through to the end result.

About three-fourths of the way up, I stop to catch my shallow breath. My right foot slips off the rock, and suddenly I'm falling. I frantically grab for anything and just by chance get hold of one of the roots coming out of the rock. I'm lucky. My right foot finds a solid rock, and I'm able to steady myself. I consider turning back, but it would probably be just as hard to go down now as go up. And though it sounds kind of silly, if I'm going to die anyway, I'd rather be going up than down.

By the time I make it to the top, the sun, as yellow as Bart Simpson's face, is fully up and in the blue sky the aliens love so much. I'm panting with doglike urgency and have the powerful thirst those energy drinks are always claiming they can satisfy. Claimed. I have to keep reminding myself. Everything is past tense.

My legs dangle over the side. I've got little cuts all over me from the uneven rock edges. I feel stupid. But then a cool breeze passes over my sweaty skin and I look out over a broad, beautiful valley and I can see all the way to Taos, and in that moment it is all worth it. All I've done to get here, to see this, to be a part of it. Survived.

Been a slave. Escaped. Run. Fought. Killed. Nearly died. This is my world. It belongs to me, and I belong to it.

The feeling blows over me like the wind. I can't hold on to it. But when it's gone, I have its memory and it gives me strength.

My dad sits next to me. (Okay, I'm not totally psycho. This isn't *Hamlet*. I know my dad isn't here, not even as a ghost. But I kind of pretend my dead father can visit me sometimes. At least I think I'm pretending. It's sort of a daydream that sometimes seems a little more real than it should.)

"Look where you've got yourself now, Grasshopper," he says. "You're free."

My dad is — was — a big man. He had blond hair that, in certain lights, seemed almost white. People said he was handsome, but I always thought it was more like his face had a lot of personality. People remember it.

"I'm not a slave anymore," I say.

"And you've got a girlfriend."

"I guess." Technically Lauren is my girlfriend, and I did feel close to her, so close, on the journey from Austin to Taos. Not so much since we made it to the rebel camp, though. I don't know why. It's disappointing.

"And you killed one of the lords."

"Yeah, and it's made people think I'm something I'm not."

"You know you're going to have to help them see."

"See what?"

"It's like before you and your friends made up your minds to escape. You wanted to believe you could just survive as slaves, didn't you? You thought you'd be lucky to do that. But then you realized you could do more. You escaped."

"We did. And a lot of people died."

"You might have never tried," he says. "You might have died a slave."

"That was totally different. We escaped. We didn't fight them. Fighting them is different. We can't win."

This is the truth that was too big to say to Doc and Running Bird and that Robert guy and even to myself. They're way more powerful than we will ever be, and there are too many of them. It's just not possible to win. We can fight, but we can't win.

"You couldn't escape, either," my dad says. "Or so you thought. Until you did, right?"

"It's not the same."

I'm looking out over the broad expanse, but when I turn to my dad to ask him what I should do, he's not there. I'm talking to myself. I'm sitting by myself.

"I hate it when you do that!" I shout.

No answer. Just the echo of my words off the rocks. Maybe that is the answer.

5

After a while, I make my way around the cliff and find
a safer way down. When I near camp, I hear voices and
see people getting breakfast and sitting at tables and eating. Someone sees me and shouts, "There he is!" Heads
turn my way. The people closest to me think, *Worried.*
Or maybe they feel worried. This whole telepathy thing
is confusing. It's like everyone is always boiling over with
thoughts and feelings, some of which are clear and dis-
tinct but most of which are vague and confusing, like
background chatter at a party.

"We thought you were lost," someone says.

I hear others agree, and the weight of their concern
embarrasses me. I look away, which is when I notice
Dylan across the clearing. He's not one of the ones

sending me waves of worry. Instead, he's busy talking to a pretty brown-haired girl who's looking at him all moon-eyed. I have this rush of images: dozens of other girls looking at him just that way and then crying over him later. *Player.*

The images go away when Dylan finally sees me. He stops talking, and his body stiffens with anger, his face swells with it. *Stay the hell out of my head, you freak,* he mindpseaks.

Guard your thoughts better, I mindspeak back.

He pushes toward me through the crowd, bumping people but either not noticing or not caring. I watch as he shields his thoughts, hiding his rage from everyone, looking outwardly concerned. Hiding from everyone except me, because I can still read him, even when he's shielded. No one else can do that.

Maybe he's right. Maybe I am a freak. I mean even more of a freak than the freaks we've all become.

"Where have you been?" Dylan says when he reaches me, his voice sounding as concerned as he looks. Even I almost believe him.

Everyone near us has stopped talking and is watching us. "Out for a walk," I say. "Seeing the sights."

"What is wrong with you?"

I think the list is practically endless, but I say, "Something is wrong with me because I took a walk? What's the big deal?"

"The big deal is you were gone when your girlfriend woke up, and she got people worried. This isn't a Boy Scout camp."

"It would be a strange one," I say.

Someone laughs, which I appreciate.

Dylan's eyes narrow. "Even the little kids know not to wander off and get lost."

"I wasn't lost," I say. "I just wanted some time to myself."

"Of course, if you really had the Warrior Spirit in you, you wouldn't get lost." He forces a smile.

"I wasn't lost." *You moron.* Too late I realize I didn't shield the thought, so it floats out into the world for all to hear.

I know the truth about you, Dylan mindspeaks.

He's thinking this just to me, blocking out everyone else. I think I see how he does it, and I file that information away. In spite of my dislike and distrust of him, I can't help listening closely, like maybe he does know some truth about me.

You aren't special. You don't know anything. You don't belong here with us, he mindspeaks.

You aren't so special, either, I retort, which I admit does have a fifth-grade ring to it.

Funny. I think of that word — *retort.* It's my mom's word. She was always on me about improving my vocabulary. Once I accidentally called her dude, and you would have thought I'd just confessed to murder. She talked for a long time about how she'd failed as a mother, how all her hard work had been for naught (yes, she used this word and lots of others like it and, yes, she could be pretty embarrassing in public — make that very embarrassing). But here I am using her word, which reminds me of her and makes me remember that a part of her is still in me. Another thing to hold on to. Another way the aliens haven't won.

Dylan struts off. I think he does something that makes him seem bigger than he is, but I don't know what. Another talent? Lauren and Catlin come up behind me as I'm trying to figure this out. I see them in my mind almost the way you'd see a shadow move out of the corner of your eye.

"You thought I was missing?" I say to Lauren, irritated she put me in a position where Dylan could chastise me in public.

"I wasn't actually worried," she says, and I can sense that she's irritated that I'm irritated. "Dylan asked me where you were, and I said you weren't in your tent when I woke up. He's the one who made a big deal about it."

"Dylan just wanted to embarrass you," Catlin says, which is exactly what I'm thinking.

"You should tell people before you go somewhere, though," Lauren says, unknowingly echoing Dylan. "It's not safe here. Or anywhere."

"Everyone's nervous after yesterday," Catlin says. "They all think something is going to happen."

"Something *is* going to happen," I say.

"Of course something is going to happen," Lauren says.

"I mean something more specific," I say.

"What do you mean?"

"Yeah, what?" Catlin says.

"I had a dream last night." I tell them about it. About the Hunter and deathdays and the Hunter's employers needing us dead before word of our telepathic abilities gets out and the endless fleet of alien ships that I saw out in space.

"Are you going to tell Doc?" Catlin asks.

I shake my head. "It was just a dream. I already told him about the smuggler, so he knows everything we know."

"But you didn't tell him about the dream," Catlin says.

"It was just a dream," Lauren says.

"Yeah," I say, "it was just a dream."

I'm glad to agree with Lauren.

"Um . . ." Catlin says.

"No um," I say.

"Sorry, but there is an um," Catlin says. "You're a dreamwalker. 'Just a dream' doesn't work for you."

Lauren frowns, which makes me frown, too.

"It could be just a dream," I insist.

"You met me in a dream. I'm pretty real, right?" Catlin says.

Small and pretty and very real. Sometimes I feel like she's the most real thing in my life. I immediately regret this thought.

"That was different," I say.

"Real is real. Dreams are dreams," Lauren says, like she is stating the obvious, which once would have been true but isn't anymore. "He can tell the difference."

"It's hard for dreamwalkers sometimes," Catlin says.

Great. On top of everything else, now it's hard for me to know what's real and what's a dream. The list of what's hard for me just keeps growing.

"Look," Lauren says, "not all dreams can be true even for someone with Jesse's—" She frowns. What to call it?

"Talent," Catlin says.

Lauren's frown deepens, because can this really be a talent? I wonder myself. "Whatever it is," she says, "it's not like every dream Jesse has is going to be real, right?"

"Your hunter sounds kind of real to me," Catlin says. "The way you said he felt powerful. The way he could sense you even though you didn't want him to. A dreamwalker is very protected in a dream; even when you were weaker, you managed to get away from Lord Vertenomous. This hunter must be incredibly powerful to have sensed you and almost destroyed you."

"But if the dream was real," Lauren says grudgingly, "then what does it tell us?"

"I don't know," Catlin says.

"It means they won't stop," I say.

"Won't stop what?"

Catlin understands. "They won't stop coming."

"They won't stop until there's no more space. They will fill our world," I say.

"Oh, my God," Lauren says. "We need to tell people. If this is going to happen, they need to know the facts so they can decide what to do. We can't fight billions. There aren't enough of us."

"There never will be enough," I say. "We could stay in those caves for a thousand years. It wouldn't matter."

"We should get Doc to allow us to talk at tonight's meeting," Lauren says decisively. She says most things decisively. It's one of the things I like about her. "The sooner people know what we're up against, the sooner we can start preparing a strategy."

"I think Jesse should tell Doc about his dream before we tell everyone else," Catlin says. "Doc is in charge."

It doesn't take a mind reader to sense what Lauren thinks, but she begrudgingly agrees. "Doc first, but everyone needs to know."

Zack, Zelda by his side, waves from across the camp where they're eating. I'm thinking I'd like to join them. I'm thinking something smells good.

"I'll go talk to Doc after breakfast," I say, returning Zack's wave.

Lauren shoots me a look. "How can you think of food at a time like this, Jesse?"

It isn't hard. I think of food pretty regularly — and other things she'd be even more disappointed to know about. I don't say any of this, though. Instead, I give Zack a helpless shrug and dutifully follow Lauren and Catlin down the main path to a smaller side path that leads to the big brown circus tent that the rebels use as a town hall.

Inside are desks, tables, and chairs and even some office-looking stuff: computers and phones and radios and a TV. The aliens systematically destroyed our machines when they invaded because, apparently, out there in the big universe there is an empire of machine worlds that they're at war with. Even though our machines are primitive, the aliens don't trust them. These are the first machines I've seen since I worked on a machine-destruction crew in the early days after the invasion.

The phones in the tent aren't cell phones; they're landlines hooked to cables, which stretch out of the tent and down the mountain toward the strange brown and white restaurant (it looks like it's made of gingerbread) at the bottom of the ski runs. I wonder if they work — and if they do, who we would even call? Is there anyone left to answer?

A woman stands in front of Doc and complains

about her neighbor. She's short and wide, with brown hair that looks like it has been chopped off with a knife. Which it probably was.

"You've got to do something. I can't sleep."

"We can move you," Doc says. "I'm afraid it would have to be to Section 4 due to the growing population."

"Oh, no, you don't. You aren't moving me out to the boonies. He's the one who snores. He should move. Could you sleep to this?"

She demonstrates the snoring with several loud snorts and a long whistle. Catlin, Lauren, and I laugh. Big mistake. The woman swings around. Unfortunately, her anger focuses on me. Both Lauren and Catlin cover their smiles with totally fake coughs.

"Something funny about my not being able to sleep, young man?"

"Not at all," I say, doing my best to smile congenially (another Mom word). "People who snore are a menace to society."

"Are you trying to be funny?"

"No, ma'am," I say, no longer smiling. Where's the Warrior Spirit now? I bet a lot of those people who want to believe I'm the Chosen One would give up hope if they saw me with this woman.

Apparently the *ma'am* works. (I'm from Texas, and we know the value of a well-placed *ma'am*.) The woman turns back to Doc.

"That man has got to be stopped. If you don't do something about him, then I will," she says ominously, and stomps out of the tent. There is a bit of a waddle to her stomp because of what my mom would have called her robust figure, but somehow it doesn't weaken her ability to intimidate. None of us laughs even after she's out of sight.

Doc lets out a long sigh. "I hope she doesn't poison him or smother him in his sleep before I can get this resolved. The problem is, the man is as stubborn as she is. I'm surprised they aren't married." He pauses. "Come to think of it, maybe they were once."

He puzzles over this for a few seconds and then waves away the thought. "Well, what can I do for you three? Someone snoring in your neighborhood, too?"

This is where I'm supposed to tell him all about my dream-that-maybe-wasn't-a-dream. But I chicken out, and instead I point to the phones. "Do those work?"

Doc nods. "The aliens took out the satellites in the first attack, but we've had some success with landlines. We've been able to talk with other survivors in Albuquerque and even, once, in San Diego. You want to make a call?"

Lauren, being Lauren, has no patience for this. She tells Doc all about my dream, but she doesn't stop there. She gives some reasons he should allow her to speak at the meeting tonight and inform the New Americans.

She expands from this into democratic principles and her disapproval of one person, no matter how benevolent he might be, being all-powerful.

"Did you not just see me dealing with Mrs. Taylor?" Doc says. "Did I look all-powerful to you?"

"You're the head of the Wind Clan, though," Lauren says.

"Actually, I'm the head of Jupiter House," he says, "and Wind Clan."

"I'm just saying New America should be different. We should be a democracy, with an elected official and an informed populace. A populace that gets to choose whether to stay and fight or to try a different approach."

If Doc is upset by what Lauren is saying, he doesn't show it. Instead, he regards her with the steady gaze of a teacher—which makes sense, given that's what he was before all this. "Perhaps sometime in the future you'll be right. Perhaps we will be able to hold elections and make New America a true democracy."

"What's wrong with now?" she says.

"We're at war," he says.

"So what? The democracy is put on hold until we defeat the aliens? And if that doesn't happen right away and you become too old to rule—or if you die in the battle—then your son inherits? It's like a monarchy."

I see Doc appreciating something he hasn't before. Lauren's telepathic abilities aren't strong, and she has no special talent, but she is talented. She's scary smart. She's a natural leader. She is relentless.

"There will be time to consider these issues in the future. I'm not on my deathbed just yet," says Doc.

I can feel the frustration radiating off Lauren like a fever. Doc adds, "As for your request to inform the people of the approaching settlers, I'm afraid I have to ask you to keep quiet about that for now."

"I don't know if I can do that."

"People are close to panic, Lauren. It would be foolish to give them more cause for alarm without knowing if this information is accurate."

Lauren doesn't look convinced. "How can we verify what Jesse saw?" she asks.

"We'll leave that up to Running Bird," Doc says.

"Why Running Bird?"

"He is talented in many ways, a priest, even if he has withdrawn his vows. He knows many hidden secrets. And he is the smartest person I know. He will help Jesse discover the truth of his dreams."

Lauren looks about as skeptical as I feel. But Catlin seems to accept what he says right away.

Doc tells me that Running Bird will find me when he's ready. In the meantime, we agree to keep the doomsday news to ourselves — which I'm more than happy to do.

6

I never do get to have breakfast. By the time Lauren, Catlin, and I leave the tent, the breakfast dishes are being put away. I hope Lauren can hear my stomach rumbling as we walk back to our campsite, but she looks too preoccupied to hear much of anything.

"I've always hated secrets," she tells me. "He's forcing us to keep secrets."

"Just for a little while," I say.

"He's like a king," she says. "This is America. New America. Whatever. It should be a democracy."

She asks Catlin if all the houses and clans are like this. Catlin doesn't know. She wasn't that interested in politics. This earns her a lecture in responsibility from Lauren. I find myself getting sleepy, and I say I'm going to rest a little in my tent. I ask Lauren if she maybe wants to catch a nap. I'm thinking a little alone nap time might help us get back to those feelings we seemed to have for each other on the trip here. She says she doesn't nap, and I can tell she doesn't approve of the whole concept of sleeping during the day.

I do. Especially considering how little sleep I've had the past few nights. I hardly lie down before I'm sound asleep, and I sleep until someone — Catlin, it turns out — wakes me.

"Running Bird said you're supposed to go to the main tent."

I roll over, but she shakes me. "Now."

I grumble about it, but I go. And then he isn't even there. I ask Doc where he is, and he doesn't know, hasn't seen him. That's when two scouts come in and tell Doc it's safe to make the run to Taos for supplies. Doc tells them to inform Dylan and the rest of the team that the mission is on.

"Tell them to meet here in five minutes," Doc says.

Since I'm there and there's no Running Bird, I ask Doc if I can go along.

"Are you sure?" Doc says.

"Yeah. I want to go." Anyway, it will get me out of meeting with Running Bird. But then I have a strange thought. What if this was why he told me to come here? How could he know when the scouts would come back, though?

When Dylan shows up, he isn't happy to hear Doc order him to take me along. "It's my team," Dylan says. "I decide who I take."

Doc says, "It will be safer with Jesse. And he could use the experience."

"Doc's right," one of the other guys says. "I saw Jesse fight. I'd feel safer if he came along."

Dylan is not happy about this, not happy at all. But others say they want me along, too. He gives in.

"Good," Doc says wearily, as though the exchange was taxing. And maybe it was. Maybe he and Dylan were engaged in some serious mindspeak that they shielded us from.

"Take your meds, old man," Dylan says. "You look like hell."

It's rude, but he's right. Doc's face looks pale and drawn. But even as I think this, the impression of weakness fades and is replaced by a healthy glow. Either my eyes are playing some serious tricks on me or Doc did something to make himself seem healthier. What powers do these people have that I don't even know about?

"Come on, then, if you're coming," Dylan says to me, and starts off down the path at a fast pace.

I start to follow but turn to catch a last look at Doc; he isn't there. In fact, I can't see the camp at all. It's disappeared.

"Doc and Running Bird put a cloaking over the

camp," a girl just in front of me says over her shoulder. "You won't be able to hear anything, either, until we get back up the path."

"They've hidden the whole camp?" I say.

"As best they can. You can't see it unless you're close or have a special talent. We're lucky Doc and Running Bird have the strength. Not many could do it over so much space."

We continue down the trail, and after about ten minutes, we get to the vehicles. The girl goes to a blue truck, and I follow her. I'd like to hear more.

"You ride with me, New Blood," Dylan says.

Lucky me, I think.

"I heard that," Dylan says.

Not surprisingly, the truck he has is one of those big trucks with big tires—the biggest truck of the three, I notice. Seeing it, I wish Lauren had come along. She might ask him what he's compensating for. It's the kind of thing she'd say and the kind of thing I'd love to hear her say.

"I'm not compensating for anything, dickhead," he says.

I put up a stronger shield. I have to admit one thing: his telepathic ability is strong, much stronger than the others with us.

Dylan drives us down the mountain. I can feel someone trying to shield the trucks, but they aren't doing a very good job. I'm about to see if I can help when Dylan interrupts my thoughts.

"You know why I don't like you?"

"You were the strongest here before I came," I say.

"You aren't stronger than me. You just think you are," he says, but I can feel his doubt, and I can also feel his hatred swell. "You're dangerous. You're going to get us killed because people think you can save us. No one can save us but us. If we hide in the caves, maybe we have a chance."

"I never said I had the Warrior Spirit in me."

"It's just a story," he says, not hearing me, "a stupid old story. My dad and Running Bird believe in all that, gods and stories. I don't." He glares at me. "You shouldn't have come. You're not one of us."

"I didn't say I was," I say.

"Good, 'cause you aren't. And you sure aren't any demigod."

"I couldn't agree more."

"But everyone else thinks you are — or a lot of people, anyway. You could help me get them to safety. Help me persuade everyone to follow me to the caves. Use what they think to do something right."

I consider telling him about the settlers, but Doc told me not to, and I trust him more than I trust Dylan.

"What's wrong with Doc?" I say instead.

He doesn't answer me at first. I think he'll ignore

me, which is fine. A little silence would be fine. Then he says, "Bad heart. He's had one heart attack already. The stress is too much. It's time for a change."

"I'm sorry."

"I don't need you to be sorry. I need you to help me get these people to a safe place."

We pass through the outskirts of Taos and into the main area of town. Taos has the eerie feel to it that towns, even small ones, have without people. Empty streets. Empty sidewalks. Empty buildings. Empty houses. The only things here are ghosts.

I feel a tightness in my chest as we near the square. This is where it happened. People's minds being snapped. Bodies dead before they hit the ground. And there's me, too, killing the great lord. Snapping his mind as he was about to snap mine.

The truck stops in front of a hotel tucked in among a row of buildings. There's a little patio out front with metal tables and chairs. I see people sitting there. For a second I'm surprised and happy—more survivors. That's when I look around and see cars going down the street and a UPS truck. I hear voices talking loudly and some-one shouting from across the square. I feel unsteady, almost like the earth is shivering beneath me. Then the people and the cars disappear. The sounds of voices die. I'm back. Back from where? Makes no sense. Then I think of Running Bird's past, present, and future talk and wonder if he did something to me, if he's playing some trick on me.

Dylan hops out of the truck, and the others do the same.

"Jamie, Susan," Dylan calls. "You're with me on food detail."

Two girls—two very pretty girls—get in the cab of Dylan's truck. To me Dylan says, "You're on *baño* detail. Get toilet paper, soap, anything we can use. Meet out front with the others in about twenty minutes."

Dylan drives off, and I turn to the guy next to me. "Where're they going?"

"Hit the restaurants and convenience stores to try to find stuff."

"Why not grocery stores?"

"Already emptied in this little town. We better get inside."

He gives me trash bags for my bathroom trip. Others are going to the hotel rooms for towels, blankets, and other supplies. I'm coming out of my sixth bathroom, with one bag full of toilet paper and the other almost full of soap and paper towels, when this girl named Angela tells me it's time to go. We all meet out front and wait for Dylan.

We're talking—someone jokes about Dylan probably having to stop at a bar to get some bottles for one of his parties—when I sense someone powerful. Someone a little ways off but too powerful to be human. Alien. He doesn't seem to know we're here. Yet.

"Alien," I say, and the illusion of safety I didn't even know I was feeling — the safety of being in a group, the safety of numbers — disappears.

7

The others are looking around nervously, but they can't sense him. I can feel the panic start to fill them, and I can feel them fighting it.

The alien and I sense each other—mentally. He's surprised that I can sense him, and I'm surprised, too. It's like the volume of my telepathic power has been turned up.

"He's on the other side of the plaza," I say.

I don't think through my actions. I run. And not away from the alien, which would be a wise strategy, but toward him. My shoes slap hard against the pavement; my breath quickens. The adrenaline is rushing through me, but everything seems to slow down. I think how I've been powerless to stop the deaths of so many. *Not this time.*

What I don't plan on is the other rebels running after me. I want to tell them to turn around and go back. But by then it's too late.

The alien is trying to hurry toward his ship so he can give other aliens our position. He's not very good at hurrying. His body jerks and strains. He looks like Big Bird trying to run after having slammed a couple of lattes. I realize something: all the aliens are like this. Their minds are graceful and fast as sharks, but their bodies are clumsy and slow. Their weakness makes me feel a little stronger.

I rush after him. My mind and body both go, but my mind is much faster. It's almost like flying. The ground blurs beneath me. I'm near the plaza; the others are far behind me. Good. I nearly run right into the alien because I can't stop myself in time. We are both surprised, like two people who unexpectedly meet rounding a dark corner at night. Neither of us moves.

Suddenly I have this memory of history class, but it seems more intense than just a memory — almost like I'm really there, back in Mr. White's class, and not just remembering it. We're studying World War I, and we're reading this private's journal. He's my age, seventeen, and he describes what it's like at Verdun in the trenches. At one point he and everyone else are ordered to attack a trench. He has to run across this muddy field while machine guns rattle off rounds and rounds of sharp little pieces of metal and powder. And all around him his friends and his fellow soldiers fall, some screaming in agony and others silent except for the thud their bodies make when they hit the mud.

These trenches aren't just like big ditches. They have barbed wire in front of them and all kinds of things that make it even harder to get through. Soldiers that do make it as far as the rolls of wire often get caught up in it, their skin ripped from their bodies as they try to untangle themselves.

The private is lucky. He's one of the few who doesn't die trying to get to the trench. Somehow he makes it across the killing field, through all those bullets and all that wire, but then he's all alone. He has no idea where he is or where the other soldiers in his unit are or if any of them are still even alive. Then the shelling starts. He can't tell if it's the enemy or his own side. It doesn't matter. There are explosions everywhere. An avalanche of dirt and sharp objects and body parts falls down on him from the sky, or it seems like it's from the sky, anyway. He lies with his hands over his head for what seems like hours. When the shelling finally stops and he looks up, he sees a German soldier lying inches away. The German soldier is as startled as the English soldier that they are in the same trench. They jump to their feet and struggle to get their mud-soaked rifles pointed at each other.

But they don't fire. Even though they are sworn

enemies and each has likely killed his share of the other's friends and fellow soldiers, neither pulls his trigger. Instead, they put down their guns and spend the night in the trench, sharing smokes, not saying much because they can't speak each other's language. The next morning they say good-bye and go their separate ways without doing what soldiers are put on battlefields to do. A day later, the English soldier sees the German soldier dead on the ground. He writes that even though the German is the enemy, he feels like he's lost another friend.

I am back to the present, and somehow I know that my little trip lasted only a fraction of a second. Like the two soldiers, the alien and I are startled to find ourselves so close, both physically and mentally now. We both have our weapons raised: our minds. We are both ready to turn the other off. But we've stopped ourselves, just like the German and the Englishman did. We don't pull our triggers.

This alien patrol is my enemy. I know that. His kind is responsible for the death of my parents, for the death of everyone I loved, for the end of our world as we know it. And yet . . .

The patrol isn't much older than I am, and he's scared. I feel that. He's scared of dying. He does not want to be here. Neither of us wants to be here, and we share this, and for a moment it's almost like we're joined—connected mentally in a way that makes it feel like we're one being instead of two, like we have more in common than I have with my fellow humans.

For a moment, I even think this alien and I might be like the English and German soldiers. I think maybe we don't have to try to kill each other. We can find a way not to.

Then the others catch up.

That's when I remember yesterday sitting on the bench at dinner and the strange daydream about this square and fighting Lord Vertenomous and then fighting another alien. This is the alien. I was in this moment. I've been in this moment before. And I was losing.

The others circle around him before I can tell them not to. Everyone is scared. Fear and panic are all around me. And anger and hate. Someone is about to attack with her mind. I can feel it, and the alien can, too. Suddenly it doesn't matter what I say or what he might say or what anyone else might say. It's gone too far, and there's no way back.

Was all this written? Did I ever have a chance to stop it?

With one swipe of his arm, the alien kills a boy next to me. The boy's face goes blank, and he drops to the ground with a thud.

I'm sorry for your loss. I think the alien means it, but it doesn't matter. He has killed, and he's going to keep killing.

I move to attack him, but he's ready and blocks me. I change tactics, and I'm able to throw him, and he flies through the air. Not him, exactly, but his mind or whatever. He's up in a second, and he grabs me and twists me, and even though my feet are firmly planted on the ground, I feel myself falling. Falling into something deep and dark that feels like there's no end to it.

I'm sorry for your loss.

At first I think this is for me, but when I twist away from the fall, the darkness fades and I'm standing on solid ground. A girl behind me is dying. Angela.

It's my fault.

I strike the alien with everything I've got—twice. He blocks both strikes but staggers.

My fault.

I need to move faster. I need to strike harder. I feel the vulnerable place in him, and I twist like I'm breaking a neck in a hapkido move, one hand on the chin and one on the opposite side of the head above the ears. I snap something in his mind. He dies.

I'm on my knees, trying to catch my breath. My body aches all over like it does after sparring in tae kwon do, like I've been physically beaten.

A truck screeches to a stop on the road, the doors swing open, and Dylan and the two girls jump out. They run over.

"Is it dead?" Dylan asks.

"He," I say, looking up at him.

He glares at me. "What?"

"He's a male."

"I don't give a shit."

"He's dead," I say.

He orders everyone to get in the trucks and to bring the dead, including the alien. He tells me, "Carry it to the truck and get in."

I don't move. The hate is still running through me, and it is too big to be just for the dead alien. I hate myself and I hate Dylan and I hate everything.

"He is not an it," I say.

One word. One more stupid word from Dylan, and I'm going to hurt him. It's the hate. The hate needs a way out. Dylan is the way. I need to hit someone, and he's the strongest one here.

"Boys, boys, boys," a girl's voice behind me says. I'm shaking, and sweat dampens the back of my neck.

The girl steps between us. She's a pretty Latina with deep brown eyes and coal-black hair, older than us by a couple of years. She's one of the stronger ones. Funny, I wouldn't have been able to tell that only a few days ago.

"Doc would want the ship," she says. "Me and the Chosen One will fly it back."

"I'm not the Chosen One," I say.

"Whatever you are, I've never seen anything like what you just did. You were moving like they move. I'd like to know how."

I keep my eyes on Dylan, but my anger has evaporated. As we walk away, Dylan says, "Okay, Sam, you fly that ship back and take the New Blood with you, but just make sure you don't make any stops along the way."

"Where would I stop, boss? You think I'm going to grab a Big Mac?"

"Funny," he says, trying to act like he's in on the joke instead of the butt of it.

Sam gives him a salute that somehow looks like she's giving him the finger. I'm not sure how she does it, but it's a skill I definitely want to learn.

"Jerk," I say.

"Careful," she says. "He'll most likely be the next leader. And he can hold a grudge."

I follow Sam into the ship. It's the first time I've been back in one of the alien ships since Lauren, Catlin, and I escaped from Austin. It was trying to steal one of these that got Michael and Lindsey killed.

"You know," Sam says, "there's a story about the Warrior taking other shapes. You took another shape back there."

"That was me," I say, trying to scoff at the idea, but

my scoffing abilities have been severely reduced. Alien invasion will do that to you.

"You're sure you can't become something else? Not even, you know, a squirrel or something?"

"I was a vampire on Halloween once," I say.

She gives me a polite smile. "You become like them when you fight, like the aliens. It's a kind of shape-shifting."

"I'm me," I say. "I was just me."

"Okay," she says. "So what are you?"

I get that question a lot, I mindspeak.

But the truth? I still don't have a good answer. Some crazy things have been happening to me. Being in the past and being in the future but at the same time being in the present. Almost like I was, am, and will be in two places at once, which is impossible.

Right?

Nothing can be in two places at once. One of the rules of the universe. But here's the thing: when the impossible keeps becoming the possible, the rules no longer seem so reliable. One plus one always equals two? Maybe. Maybe not.

What am I? I don't know.

Sam doesn't fly much better than Catlin, who flew us out of Austin with a ship we stole but sort of wrecked it along the way. On our takeoff, we run into the top branches of a tree. Fortunately, we hit where they're thin, and they whip harmlessly against the ship. We rise a few hundred yards into the air.

"That was kind of close," I can't help pointing out.

"I'll tell you what I tell everyone who complains about my flying. If you think you can do better, here's the control."

She takes her hand off the control, and the ship drops. My stomach drops with it. She smiles. It's a beautiful smile, though I'm unable to fully appreciate it because — hello — we're dropping to our deaths.

"No," I say, gripping my seat.

"No what?"

"No, I don't want to fly."

We're still dropping. In fact, we're dropping even faster, it seems, or maybe the earth is just coming up to meet us.

"If you're sure . . ." she says.

"I'm sure!" I shout.

She puts her hand on the control, and we swoop up and away from the unforgiving earth. I keep gripping the seat. I have to consciously convince my fingers to let go. "You're kind of crazy, aren't you?" I say.

"Takes one to know one," she says. "Sit back and enjoy the ride."

Enjoy the ride? Not so much. We jerk up and down several times, like we're caught in air currents. While I don't pretend to have Lauren's brilliant mind, I am capable of learning from my mistakes; not one word of criticism escapes from my lips.

"Where are we going, anyway?" I ask.

"Little place about halfway between here and camp. We stored the other ship we took from the aliens in the barn there. This gives us two. Practically an air force."

"Two ships is an air force?"

"I said practically."

"In Austin we saw thousands of alien ships."

"Really?" she says. "Think they'd lend us a few?"

"If we force them to."

"Now you're thinking like someone who has the spirit of the Warrior in him. If we want ships, we should go get them. I like it."

"I didn't say that," I say.

"Can I ask you something?" Sam says after a while.

"Sure," I say, expecting a question about the ships.

"Did you hesitate?" The question catches me off-guard, but she mistakes my discomfort for confusion. "It felt like you hesitated when you and the alien faced off," she explains.

I want to tell her about my memory from history class about the World War I soldiers or my guilt about killing even someone as terrible as Lord Vertenomous or my feeling that the alien boy didn't want to be there any more than I did. I don't, though. I answer her question. "Yes."

What she says next she says softly, but it's not soft. It's not soft at all. "And two people died."

"He didn't want to kill us any more than I wanted to kill him," I say. "I felt that."

"You can't hesitate," she says, like what I just said doesn't matter at all. And maybe it doesn't, or it shouldn't. I don't know anymore. "I get that this is hard for you," she continues. "You're not a soldier. You're just a kid. I get it, but if you hesitate, more will die. You'll let more die."

More will die. Because of me.

"This is war, Jesse. Maybe you've got the Warrior Spirit in you, maybe not. But you can fight like they fight. It's a talent. You have to use it."

Being able to kill is my talent. Why can't I just hear really well, like Zelda? Or why can't I be a healer, like Catlin? Help people. Save people.

"You *can* save people," Sam says, startling me. I put my shield back up. "You need to start acting like a leader, Jesse, because we need you."

"Intercourse," I mutter.

"Excuse me?" Sam says, with knife-blade sharpness.

"I didn't mean . . . I wasn't asking you. . . . I mean . . . it's my mom's fault."

Her expression does not soften when I blame my mother.

I tell her, the words rushing out, about my mom being an English teacher and convincing my father and me to use alternative methods of swearing rather than relying on swear words, which she said were reductive and stunted our vocabularies.

Sam shakes her head. "You are one lame Chosen One." She sounds so much like Michael just then that she brings him back to me, and I miss him in that sudden and hard way that loss has of filling and emptying you at the same time. Then I try not to think about him because it hurts.

"I tried to tell you," I say.

"You did."

"Of course, some people seem to think I'm, you know, part god now," I say. "A demigod."

"I don't think so."

"But you don't know. No one knows."

She takes her hands off the controls again. We drop, very quickly and with increasing momentum.

"Any god, even a part god, should be able to make one of these ships rise, right? Can you do that?"

"No," I say. When she doesn't put her hand back on the control, I quickly add, "I said no. No. No. No. No."

She smiles and takes back control of the ship.

"I really hate it when you do that," I tell her.

She doesn't seem too worried about my displeasure—or worried at all. You'd think a possible demigod, even one who can't stop ships from falling, would inspire a little more respect, but I decide against bringing this up. In fact, I sort of make a rule that I won't bring up much of anything with Sam unless we're on the ground.

There's a truck in the barn where the other ship is, so Sam lands and I get out and move it so Sam can take the ship in and park it next to the other ship. It's a tight squeeze, but she manages. By the time we're done, the rest of the search party has caught up to us, and we all drive together to the ski lodge and park the cars and trucks where we got them. Then we hike with the others up the trail to camp. We get as far as the town hall circus tent before Robert stops us and says Doc needs to be debriefed.

"Debriefed?" I say. "What are we, spies?"

Sam gives me a withering look.

"We're soldiers," Sam says. "You'd better get used to taking orders, Chosen One."

Quit calling me that, I mindspeak.

Whatever you say, Chosen One, she mindspeaks back.

We go inside the tent, and Dylan gives Doc a full report. Afterward, Doc tells Sam and me to stay. He wants to know all about the fight, how I fought. I find it hard to put into words. I tell him that the moves seemed physical to me somehow. My mind turns them into moves I've done in tae kwon do and hapkido and judo.

"They can't be real, though," I say. "I mean, my mind is doing something, not my body."

"What is real, exactly?" Doc says.

Sam says, "When the conversation starts going all wobbly at the knees, I'm out of here. Call me when you need me."

Off she goes. I take a seat in one of the metal folding chairs in front of Doc's desk.

"A lovely girl," Doc says.

Lovely isn't exactly the word I'd use, but I have to admit she's something.

"Another ship will be very helpful," he says.

I hesitate. Sam didn't mention our brilliant steal-a-fleet-of-ships-from-the-alien-headquarters-in-Austin plan, which makes me wonder if she was serious about it.

But there's no use trying to hide my thoughts from Doc.

"Out of the question," he says before I've spoken a word. "They'll be heavily guarded."

"We have to do something," I say. "Something that makes them see us."

I know I'm right as soon as I say it. We have to make the aliens see us. The aliens who are not part of the company or whatever it is. Those aliens who would care that we can hear. That we can dreamwalk. Or I can, anyway. We need them to know about us.

"It's too risky," Doc says.

"We could train for it," I say, surprising myself. "I could teach people how to fight, and Sam could teach them how to fly."

"They're too strong."

"We've got to make them see us," I repeat. "We've got to do it before they start landing more settlers. The company knows we're not product and they don't care, but from what the smuggler told me, some of the other Sans *would* care. They wouldn't settle here if they knew."

"That's assuming that these settlers are, indeed, coming," Doc says.

I start to protest, but he holds up a hand. "I'll think about it," he says. "In the meantime, I would like you to do something for me."

"Sure," I say without thinking. I know better. Saying "sure" without thinking can lead to bad places.

"I want you to sweat with Running Bird," says Doc. "He is ready."

"Sweat with him?"

"In his sweat lodge."

"I don't really need to sweat. I've been sweating a lot."

"Running Bird believes you have the Warrior Spirit in you. He's a powerful priest in the House of Jupiter, and if he believes it, then it's probably true. But I need to know. I need to know what you are, Jesse."

I'd like to know what I am, I think.

"Good man," he says. "Follow the path you took this morning, but take the very narrow path to the right just before that cliff you foolishly climbed. It will lead you to Running Bird's sweat lodge."

Someone else comes in, a guy about my age or a little older. He speaks to Doc in Spanish, and Doc rattles off Spanish back. Doc waves as I leave. I'm halfway to the path before I wonder how he knows I climbed that cliff. Maybe he read it in my mind even though I wasn't thinking about it. Or maybe he has someone watching me.

I do a quick search with my mind. No one. I'm probably just being paranoid. Still, as I pass through camp and beyond it up the mountain, I keep looking around just to make sure no one is following. As my dad used to say, it's only paranoia if it's not true.

I'm so fixated on the task that when the memory comes I nearly slip, because it's like I walk right into it. Physically I'm standing on the path just a few yards from

Running Bird's sweat lodge — I think. But mentally, I'm pulled back to the circus. It's like I'm in two places at once again.

I felt bad for the animals because they were locked in cages. The cats were especially disturbing because of the way they paced back and forth and back and forth. You could see they longed to run. You could see how their bodies were made to run somewhere, but the best they could do was pace, and that best wasn't enough. Anyone could see that. Not near enough.

They weren't the only ones who looked like they longed to be free, though. The monkeys swung restlessly around in their cages. The elephants stomped their mammoth legs, which were chained to each other.

I wanted to swing open the doors and unlock the chains and set them all free. I wanted to do something to help them.

"And where would they go?" a man next to me said. He was tall with long white hair tied back in a ponytail and very blue eyes. My parents were nearby, maybe over at a shooting booth, where my dad would be winning every stuffed animal he wanted, but I couldn't see them.

"Anywhere," I said, almost a whisper, because I wasn't supposed to talk to strangers, and if this man wasn't a stranger, I didn't know who was.

Those eyes seemed to look right through me. He was

three or four feet away, but he still seemed too close. He was like fire, radiating something that required distance to feel comfortable.

"They've been in these cages for a long time," he said. "They're used to them. That's what happens, you know. They get used to them. What good would it do if you or I went around and opened those cages?"

I was surprised that he was taking me seriously. I found myself feeling less scared of him.

"They would be free," I said.

"Perhaps. But for how long? What do you think would happen—what would *really* happen—to these animals if they were released right now?"

I understood what he was saying, but the injustice of it all made me stubborn. "They shouldn't be there."

He nodded sadly. "It's one of those problems that can't be solved by two people at a circus."

People? I was just a kid. No one had ever called me people before.

Once again, the man seemed to know what I was thinking. "Even *many* people couldn't solve this problem," he said. "Some problems grow so big it takes something just as big to solve them. You'll understand that someday. You'll have to."

The man contemplated the cages for a while in silence. "But maybe we can open just one cage."

They had these sheepdogs they used to begin a show,

seven of them. Their long, moppy hair hung over their eyes, and they had these funny expressions, as if they had a joke to tell you. They were locked in a cage, too, just like all the other animals. The man walked over to that cage, and the lock came undone at his touch. The cage door swung open.

It was like magic. Like something out of Harry Potter. That's what I thought at the time.

"Go have some fun, my pets!" he shouted.

Sheepdogs, as I'd learn later when our family got one, are naturally gregarious. They didn't need a second invitation. They bounded from their cage and out into the crowd, where they greeted and knocked over almost everyone and everything they came in contact with. They had a wonderful time.

The man looked at me but didn't speak. I mean, his mouth didn't move. *You will forget me. You will think I was a dream, but I'm a traveler. I'm from another moment many moments away from this one. I've seen you fighting gods when you are older, so I'm glad to be in this moment and see you as a boy. One day you'll wake. And you will fight gods. And you will travel. And you will be the one to make the great choice to end or begin all choices for your kind. This I see. This is my prophecy and also my memory.*

My mom and dad came over as the dogs ran off farther into the crowd, my mom carrying a large stuffed bear.

"Did you see those dogs?" my mom asked.

I nodded. "The man set them loose."

"What man?" my father said.

I pointed where the man had been, but he wasn't there anymore. No one was.

The man was right. A day, a week later, I thought that he must have been a dream. People didn't talk without voices. Everyone knew that. And who fights gods? I mean, outside of stories. It was too strange. I decided before long that I'd fallen asleep and dreamed. Then I forgot him. I forgot him just like he said I would.

I'm back to being in one place, on the path again. But I remember him now. The man from the circus. Where did he come from? And when?

I think of what Running Bird said before, about everything happening simultaneously or whatever. Does that mean that right now the moment at the circus is happening somewhere—or some*when*—else?

Fighting gods? A traveler from where and when? And what did/does he mean, I will be the one who will make the choice to begin or end all choices? I would like to blame the memory on Running Bird, who, I know, is nearby. But it's my memory. It happened long ago. The traveler said one day I would wake. Is this what he meant?

(((((10)))))

"You lost again?" Running Bird says as the path disappears in a rocky slope. He's above me, where the slope levels before a second, steeper slope.

"I wasn't lost the first time."

Running Bird smiles. His smile reminds me of the Road Runner's—a big birdie smile. It's like he is always laughing at some private joke. When Running Bird looks at me that way, I feel like I'm the joke.

"So you've come to sweat."

"And you've come to tell me if I'm a god or not."

"Demigod," Running Bird says without a trace of sarcasm.

I don't hear her coming up behind me, but I sense her. She reaches me just as I make it to the lodge. I turn around to greet her but am surprised when she jumps up and wraps her arms around my neck. I forget how small she is. In my mind there's something that makes her large, but she's light, easy to hold in my arms.

"I was so worried about you," Catlin says. "At first we didn't know who'd been killed in town. We just heard it was a boy."

"And two girls," I say because they're on my mind. My fault.

I remember the first time I saw Catlin, in a dream. She was sitting on that bed in the room where Lord Vertenomous kept her. A very pretty girl—delicate, I thought. Long blond hair, small face, long neck, arms, legs. Michael called her my dream girl. She wasn't, of course. She's real. She's right here.

"I'm okay," I say, unhooking her arms and setting her down on the flat rock.

"Sorry," she says, and blushes. "I was just worried."

I'm about to ask how she found me when Running Bird says, "Time to sweat, Warrior Boy. You come, too, little girl. This boy may need medical attention. We're going extreme with our sweat."

"I'm not a little girl, old man," Catlin says. She glares at him. She only *looks* delicate.

"You want to come or not?" he asks.

"Okay," she says, "but don't call me little girl."

"Guess I can't go naked if you come," he says.

"Please." I turn to Catlin. "Come."

Running Bird calls me homophobic. He says that nudity is the natural state of man. Clothes are artificial.

"I'm not homophobic. I just don't want to see a fat old man without clothes," I say. "I'm fat-naked-old-man phobic, maybe."

Catlin says, "Me, too."

"Okay," Running Bird says. "We'll keep some clothes on. Always good to have a cute girl in the sweat lodge. Makes the heat less painful. It's still going to be plenty painful, especially for the white boy. But less if he has his girlfriend in there."

"She's not—" I say.

"I'm not—" she says.

We both stop because we're talking at the same time, and then we're both embarrassed and confused about the embarrassment.

"Let's go," he says, and there's that Road Runner smile again.

We follow him over to the sweat lodge, which is sort of like a giant beehive set back in a crevice between two large slabs of rock—a hidden place. The ground is uneven, and piles of fallen stones are scattered here and there. A small stream trickles through the hidden place. There's a fire, a big one with a ring of rocks around it and several flat, smooth river stones in it. How can he have a fire in this no-fire zone? Then I realize that, because of the way the cliffs hang over the crevice and the caves up there, the smoke never makes it to the sky. It's drawn into the caves. This place has been chosen carefully.

"You two go sit over there while I get the ancestors ready."

"What ancestors?" I say anxiously. I half expect a gaggle of old naked men to appear, all ready for a good sweat.

He points at the stones in the fire.

"Ancestors are going to make us sweat. What is family for, anyway?"

I watch as Running Bird uses big iron tongs to take rocks from the fire and pile them inside the beehive. When he's satisfied with the pile, he sprinkles water on it and closes the tent flap.

"It's going to be like a sauna, I guess," I say, kind of hoping he'll confirm this so I'll know what to expect, though I'm not exactly a big fan of saunas. I mean, I'll sweat if there's a reason, but I don't see any point to sitting around just to sweat.

"Like a match is like a forest fire, white boy," he says.

There's a hole in the mud side of the sweat lodge, and I feel heat coming out. I say, "Is that to cool it down a little?"

"Good eye," he says, and then he puts rocks where the smoke is escaping to hold it in. Not the response I'm looking for.

"Don't people," I say, "die of heatstroke?"

"What does not break the back makes it stronger. You ever heard that?"

"Yeah," I say. That was one of my dad's sayings, and I've heard it way too many times in my life. "I've heard that. I wasn't really worried about my back."

"You got the Warrior Spirit to protect you, Chosen One."

"Not so sure about that," I say.

"And we got us a healer," Running Bird says. "She can probably bring you back."

"Probably," Catlin says, smiling that little crooked smile of hers. It's a smile that isn't quite a smile, or a smile that has something else in it that isn't a smile. So why do I like it so much?

Running Bird actually high-fives her. He practically has to get down on his knees to do it, she's so much shorter than he is.

"You need this," Catlin says to me. "You need to sweat."

I need it? I can think of a lot of things I need I'd put ahead of a sweat. A cheeseburger and fries would be way ahead of a sweat. Anyway, I'm fine. I killed an alien. He would have killed me and everyone I was with, so I killed him. I'm fine with it. Well, not fine, exactly, but okay. Well, not okay, exactly.

Fighting with gods, the man from the circus said. The aliens aren't gods, though. They're a long way from gods.

"Come on, girls and boys," Running Bird says, taking off his T-shirt and revealing powerful shoulders and arms and a substantial muffin-top stomach hanging over his jeans. "Time to sweat. Strip down to undies, and let's get going."

So we do, and I have to admit at least one good thing comes from being here: I get to see Catlin in underwear. She is hot. Not that I'm looking, except in the way that any guy, even a guy with a sort-of girlfriend, would look. I appreciate hotness. Who doesn't? Catlin has some cool tats. She has what look like Japanese symbols on her shoulder and a sunrise on her lower back just above her underwear line.

When she catches me looking at her, she smiles that not-quite-smile of hers. I smile back without thinking. Then I feel like I'm doing something wrong even though I haven't done anything wrong.

"Let's get this over with," I say to Running Bird.

We step into the sweat lodge. It's like stepping into a furnace. My face feels like it's on fire. I can't breathe. As I try to draw in a breath, something gets caught in my throat, and I try to cough it up, but I can't. I'm like a cat with a hair ball. When I finally get that under control, I realize I can't see anything because it's so dark. I'm about to run from the tent because I'm a sane person — well, mostly — and this seems like a sane response to burning heat and fire, when Running Bird mindspeaks to me.

Control your pain, Warrior Boy. You have to breathe another way, avoid the heat. Breathe another way.

This reminds me of the dojo and working out with Grandmaster Kim.

"Control breathing!" he'd shout, his heavy Korean accent booming in the small, closed room. "Control pain!"

He was big on controlling your pain.

I can't see with my eyes, but it turns out I can see with my mind, sort of. I find my way to a place next to Catlin. I feel her struggling like me. Her mind touches mine, and we both pull back. All of a sudden, after all we've been through, we're shy with each other. Maybe because we're in our underwear. Of course it's because we're in our underwear. I'm an idiot.

Running Bird starts chanting in a language I've never heard before. Then he sings. He has a surprisingly good voice. It's getting hotter and hotter in the sweat lodge.

He sprinkles more water on the ancestors. This intensifies the heat, which I wouldn't have thought possible. These are not benevolent ancestors. They have a mean streak.

Fortunately, Running Bird hands me a gallon jug of water. That helps a little, though several times I feel like I'm going to pass out. I'm surprised I don't.

"Got to let yourself go, Warrior Boy. You're fighting it. You're here now, but you have been here before and will be here again. Don't make distinctions among the three. You can dreamwalk without being asleep if you don't make the distinctions."

Crazy talk from the crazy man, but I try anyway. I use some of the meditation techniques from my martial-arts training, and suddenly I'm floating like I'm on the surface of water. Floating. Floating. I feel better, more relaxed.

"That's right," Running Bird says. "Now look at me. Follow me."

I keep my eyes closed; it's a different kind of seeing he means. I watch the way his mind pushes away from all that's around him, like pushing off from the wall of a pool. I do the same.

He floats. I float. We're not in a pool, though. It's more like a big blue lake. It feels good. It feels like I'm there instead of in the oven-like sweat lodge.

I think back to that day at the circus again and that man. For a second it's like I'm standing there beside my younger self and the man. Then something very freaky happens. The man turns to me.

"You have always been stronger than you think," he says. "It is written, but you have a choice."

I fall back—trip, I guess—and I'm back in the sweat lodge, sweating. Not floating anymore. Breathless and afraid—though I don't know of what. I try to control my breathing again, slow it. Did I fall asleep? It feels like maybe I fell asleep. Honestly, though, it also feels like maybe I didn't.

I try to see Catlin through the dark. I can see her in my mind: eyes closed, all one hundred pounds of her focused. Running Bird says it's time for a break. He needs more ancestors, hotter ones.

We go outside. The air feels cool and soft against my skin. It tastes sweet, and then I hear a bird singing. A bird. The sound is familiar and strange at the same time.

Running Bird has several plastic gallon jugs of water in a row by the tent, and Catlin and I take one and drink like we're dying of thirst, which we might be. Running Bird starts getting more stones from the fire and carrying them with the big tongs into the sweat lodge.

"Those ancestors must be angry about something," I say.

"You know what I was thinking about in there?" Catlin says.

"How can I sneak out of here?" I say.

The almost smile.

"That day you found me," she says.

Lord Vertenomous had Catlin locked away in a room. No one knew she was there until I heard her crying and saw her in a dream.

"I was lucky to find you," I say.

"You saved me."

"I did what anyone would do."

She shook her head. "You risked everything to save me."

Embarrassed, I change the subject. "Did you, by any chance, see anything while we were in there?"

"A lot of darkness. What did you see?"

"Me?" I say. "The same. I mean, hard to see much else, right?"

I try to sound normal. The fact that I have to make an effort, though, is probably a bad sign. Although it could be a good sign that I know it's a bad sign.

"Ancestors ready," Running Bird says way sooner than I want him to. "Pretty girl has to watch from the outside this time."

"Then I'm putting my clothes back on," she says.

"Better if you don't," Running Bird says. "Thinking of you out here in your underwear will give us inspiration."

"I'm getting dressed," she says, and starts putting on clothes.

Running Bird shrugs. "Sorry, Warrior Boy. You're just going to have to inspire yourself."

"Inspire myself to do what?"

"I think you know."

He motions for me to go into the sweat lodge before him. Once I get back in, I feel bad again, as bad as before. I have to struggle not to run outside all over again. I'd gotten used to being able to breathe without suffocatingly intense heat. Imagine that.

Finally, though, I do start to feel better again. Then I start to float. I have to admit, reluctantly, that it's a little easier than last time.

"Running Bird?" I say.

"You're here and before here and after here," he tells me. "Words keep trying to give order, but you can't let them. Be all places at all times. This is the way."

"It's a pretty confusing way," I say, because, come on, who could understand that? The heat just keeps getting stronger and stronger. I imagine a giant python coiling around me and squeezing. Not a good thought. I cough convulsively until my throat is so sore I can't cough anymore. I say, "Just tell me where you want me to be."

"Dreamwalk, only don't dream. Same place but different."

I'm beginning to realize that Running Bird isn't capable of a straight answer. All of his answers are bent.

"Beep beep," he says, and mindspeaks, *Walk. We walk together.*

I try to do what he says. I try to dreamwalk without dreaming, and I end up in a very strange place, a place I know and don't know. What I mean is I've seen it on TV and online, but never in real life. I'm in a Road Runner cartoon.

A Road Runner cartoon! I can't decide if I'm awed or freaked.

Or maybe equal parts both.

The land is bright yellow and the sky bright blue, with some puffy white clouds. The road is gray, and I'm on that road as the Road Runner whizzes by. Behind him is Wile E. Coyote, chasing him in a dragster. They go up a red mountain that has a road all the way around it like a coiled spring.

At the top, the Road Runner stops. It's the end of the road. Beyond that is a long, long fall. He stops very suddenly in his typical Road Runner way, all springy like. Wile E. Coyote, unable to stop in time, drives his dragster right off the cliff. Fortunately, there's a parachute. Unfortunately, it doesn't work, and the car doesn't hold together, and Wile E. Coyote, holding only the steering wheel, plummets to the earth faster than the rest of the car. Naturally the car lands on top of him, adding insult to injury. This adds more *injury* to injury, too, of course.

I wonder how it all started between them — if there is a reason the Coyote feels like he has to kill the Road Runner, besides just the fact that they exist here in this world and the Road Runner runs by him all the time and taunts him with that irritating *beep beep*. That could be enough. It could totally be enough.

Still, there's got to be an easier meal somewhere in this desert. Someone should tell him that. Of course, I guess there wouldn't be a cartoon then. The show would be over. One day the Coyote and the Road Runner learn to live in peace, THE END.

I hear Michael tell me to shut up. The first time he told me to shut up was when we got put on the same destruction crew, when the aliens had us tear everything down. Then he and I got chosen to go to Lord Vertenomous's palace to be his personal slaves because we had some of the telepathic power the aliens value so much. He told me to shut up many times there. It got so I'd try to find ways to make him say it. I smile, remembering.

Then I see the dust rising off the road beyond the cartoon hill, and I know the Road Runner is coming again. I can see the Coyote up at the top of the next hill. He's strung a trip wire across the road. On both ends of the wire are boxes marked TNT. He's hiding behind a rock with a control button in his hand.

Of course I know what's going to happen. Anyone who has ever watched the cartoon knows. Somehow the TNT is going to blow up the Coyote instead of the Road Runner.

But that's not what happens. What happens is the Road Runner runs into the trip wire. The explosives go off. The Road Runner is transformed into something that looks like a cooked turkey in a pan. The Coyote comes out from behind the rock, looking dazed. He can't believe it. Then a big smile comes over his face.

Something is wrong. The Road Runner is not supposed to die.

"You killed me!" Running Bird says to me.

"I didn't. I—"

He laughs. "That's a joke. *You* didn't kill me, because you can't cause what you can't cause, which is everything since all is written. But I'm still dead."

"We're in a cartoon," I say, shaken. "The Big Book isn't a comic book, is it?"

"This is your way of seeing this message. It's not always easy to know what messages mean, but this one seems pretty clear."

"It doesn't mean anything," I say.

"It's okay. I told you. Everything is and was and will be. I'll still be alive in some moments even if I'm dead in others. It's life. And death."

"It's crazy."

"Yes, it is. Your vision is vivid. Very strong. Might be you're getting help. Might be the Warrior Spirit is in you. Maybe he even visited you long ago and said you'd be fighting aliens?"

"No," I said.

"You sure? The Warrior Spirit might see them as something else. He's only half-god, you know. Might have thought you'd be fighting gods or other spirits."

"So you're saying he's in me? You feel him in me?"

"Might be."

"Might be?" I say. "I thought you were finally going to tell me something."

"We're going to join and see if we can read some helpful message in an immediate way. Something that might tell us how to live our next few thousand thousand moments. Maybe that will help me be sure."

I'd like to say "No, thanks," but I'm feeling guilty because of what I just saw—whether it was my fault or not.

"Fine," I say. "Lead on."

He does. He leads on. I follow.

«««((11))»»»

We're back at Lord Vertenomous's palace again, which is not a good idea, but I can't—we can't—control our walks. I can feel what it was like being here, feel the way I was afraid, feel how powerless I was when I was a slave. Any order the aliens gave I would have to follow. Go to bed. Get up. Eat. Talk. Don't talk. Before the aliens came, I sometimes felt like people were telling me what to do all the time, but when I was a slave, I realized how much freedom I'd had. When it is all taken away, you see things differently. A slave has nothing. I had nothing.

We're downstairs, and I realize that I've moved through time. I'm at a moment I've been in before. I see myself sitting at a table, eating. There are people with me, and people at other tables, too. I see Betty get up and walk over to Anchise, the psycho alien handler. I shout, "No, Betty!" while the other me whispers it because we both know what's about to happen. She slaps Anchise, and he kills her. But she blocks him once. I remember how seeing her do this made me realize they, the aliens, weren't invincible. We'd thought they were after all they'd done, but Betty's slap was the sound that woke me up. We could fight. They would probably squash us like bugs, but they weren't invincible. They weren't gods.

"Why are we here?" I say to Running Bird.

"Don't know. Sometimes we don't. Sometimes we do."

"I couldn't save her. Not then and not now."

"It's already happened."

"What use is dreamwalking, then?" I say.

"Sometimes no use," he says, shrugging, and I feel something dark and heavy trying to pull him down. It is so dark and so heavy that I can't imagine how he can carry it, but he does. "Sometimes, like when you saw the alien fleet, a dreamwalk can be important. Knowing things is sometimes important."

"Dreamwalking failed you once, didn't it?" I say. "With your wife?"

He doesn't speak right away. When he does, his voice is soft. "Saw her die but saw it too late. It was already written in the book. It happened a long time ago. Many years to me, anyway."

"I'm sorry."

"She's alive in some moments, you know. I see her every once in a while."

"I'm still sorry," I say, because I know now what it means to lose people, and I know no matter what he says, it hurts. It hurts him still after all these years.

"Your friend was very brave," he says.

"Betty," I say. "Her name was Betty."

Then everyone disappears and the lights dim and there's dust on the tables and I know I'm where I was last night with the Hunter. Same place. Different time.

"Someone very powerful is here," Running Bird says.

"Alien," I say. "The Hunter."

"It's not good for the hunted to be where the hunters are," Running Bird points out.

"You're the guide," I say.

"You're guiding now," he says. "Why are we here? Are you lost again?"

"I wasn't lost this morning. I have a good sense of direction."

"Stay focused, Warrior Boy. This is a dangerous place."

Just then I hear a familiar voice. But it's not the Hunter's. "Tex. Is that you?" it says.

"Who is that?" Running Bird says. I can feel his mind stretching in all directions, searching for the voice.

"Michael?" I say.

"About time, Tex. Where you been?"

"But you're dead," I say. I turn to Running Bird. "Can we talk to the dead when we're, you know, dreamwalking?"

"Never have," Running Bird says. Again I feel the darkness pulling at him. "Many things are possible in this universe, though. Maybe you're in a moment when the boy was alive."

"Are you dead, Michael?" I say.

"Hell, no, I'm not dead."

"Where are you?"

"I'm in some kind of cell. That hunter put me here. Now's your chance to save me the way you saved your dream girl, Tex."

He's talking about Catlin. Only Michael knew about the dream girl thing—Catlin, the girl from my literal dreams. It has to be him. Suddenly I hear doors slamming shut, the clicking of locks.

"That can't be good," I say.

"Welcome to my humble home," the Hunter says.

There's noplace to go. Every door is locked. I know this.

Somehow Running Bird makes a trapdoor in the floor. He pulls it open and shoves me through it and follows.

We fall.

· · • • · ·

We land back in the sweat lodge.

"Go get water," Running Bird rasps.

I can feel that he's weak. Making that door took a lot of power, and he's totally drained. I fumble in the dark and finally grab a gallon of water and hand it to him. He takes a long drink. He passes it to me, and I take a drink and pass it back.

"How much of that really happened?" I say. The heat closes around me. The ancestors feel angry, and there's a sour smell.

"All of it," he says.

"I can travel through time? That's real, my traveling?"

"You can be in different moments. Only the strongest dreamwalkers can be in different moments. It may happen only once or twice in a lifetime. The Warrior Spirit maybe makes it possible for you."

"But—"

"More water," he says, and I hear the weariness in his voice.

I go out of the sweat lodge and grab another gallon jug. Running Bird follows me out and motions for me to get my own jug. I do and immediately chug half of it. I'm confused, but the coolness of the air and the water make me feel better almost right away. I'm alive. I'm lucky. Still lucky.

Catlin watches us from a rock, her legs pulled up so

that her knees are pointed at the sky, her arms wrapped around them.

"What happened?" she says.

"The Chosen One dreamwalked us into a trap," Running Bird says.

I say, "We were back at Lord Vertenomous's. I heard Michael."

"You heard something," Running Bird says, taking another long drink from a gallon jug, "but I don't know if it was real. Neither do you."

"We saw him die," Catlin says.

Could it have been a trick — maybe the Hunter mimicking Michael's voice and attitude? Because she's right: we saw Michael die. I did. Saw him running across the lawn. Saw the alien. Saw him fall. Saw . . .

"We saw them take him," I say. "We thought he was dead, but what if they didn't kill him? He called me Tex in the dreamwalk. No one else calls me Tex."

"I saw him die," Catlin insists.

We saw him fall. I open up my thinking to Catlin. I show her what I remember seeing.

"Maybe," she says. "Maybe."

Running Bird says, "If he is alive, then this hunter is using him as bait. He's planning on catching you. He'll have you mounted on his wall."

"He'll have to catch me first."

"We were lucky this time. The great hunter underestimated his prey. He won't be so careless twice."

"Michael was—is—my best friend," I say. "I can't leave him there."

"You can," Running Bird says.

But he's wrong.

12

Catlin and I decide not to take the path down the mountain. We cut through the dense wood, so dark in places it might be night. The silence is immense but broken by the sound of an alien ship passing overhead. We instinctively crouch, though we're well hidden. We join without meaning to, creating a shield that the aliens can't see through — cool, but not really necessary in the thick woods. Both our faces flush at the ease of our joining. We walk on and try to pretend it didn't happen.

After a while we come to a small, grassy meadow filled with purple flowers.

"Beautiful," Catlin says. "A good place for a talk, don't you think?" She smiles that not-quite-smile of hers, and I wonder if the rest of her smile will ever come back or if her smile has always been this way, even before the invasion. There's a lot I don't know about her.

As we walk through the meadow, I tell her everything. About the dreamwalk and the Road Runner cartoon and the Hunter.

"What are you going to do about Michael?" Catlin says, and something in the way she asks makes me think she already knows.

"Who says I'm going to do anything?" Sweat beads on my face and neck from the sun. The open field is much warmer than the woods. I'm surprised I have enough liquid to make sweat after Running Bird's sweat lodge.

"You have that look."

"What look?"

"That 'I'm going to do something stupid' look."

"Oh," I say. "That look."

Amazing how quickly some people learn to identify your looks, particularly ones you'd rather they didn't.

We finish crossing the meadow and are back in the forest, the trees less dense here.

"You can't go back," she says.

She's walking faster now. She's not being careful about holding the branches until I can grab them, either. In fact, it almost seems like she's aiming some of them at me. A whip of leaves slaps my face.

"Hey," I say.

"You are so stupid," she says, and stops so abruptly that I practically run into her. Then she spins around and stomps her foot. "You'll get yourself killed."

We are very close to each other. Somehow we're leaning toward each other even. I don't know how we got so close. Then she punches me. Hard. It's a pretty good punch—though technically a low blow. She would be disqualified in a boxing match.

Pain shoots through my groin, and the breath goes out of me. I lean over, hands on knees, and take deep breaths as the pain recedes.

Stupid! she mindshouts at me as she pushes her way through the forest.

"You're stupid, too!" I shout. Okay, not the most mature or inspired comeback, but I am happy to hear my voice hasn't been raised a couple of octaves.

Once I can stand up, I think about going after her, but I don't. I decide that I need to find Lauren. That's who I need to talk to. That's who I should have told first anyway, not Catlin.

13

I find Lauren in the eating area. She's sitting at one of the picnic tables. She has a yellow notepad in front of her that's filled with her writing, which is neat and small. She looks up and smiles at me and tells me she's been working on what she calls our presentation, our five minutes to speak at the town meeting that night.

"I wasn't really thinking of it as a presentation," I say.

"Organization wins political campaigns," she says. "And that's what this is. We've got to get organized. We've got to convince people that staying and fighting is the best choice. I think we should call ourselves SAF. It's kind of catchy, don't you think?"

"I guess."

"Come on, Jesse. Show a little enthusiasm. This is our future now. There's no Yale or Harvard for us."

I'm about to tell her that there was never a Yale or Harvard for me, and I'd never wanted there to be. I don't say that, though. I don't tell her how little enthusiasm I have for speaking in front of people at the town meeting, either. Instead I say, "Michael's alive."

"Michael?" she says. I can see it takes her a few seconds to even know who I'm talking about. "Our Michael?"

"Yes."

"How? He's here?"

She looks around. She starts to smile. She has a pretty smile. It's never tentative or half a smile. Well, she has two kinds of smiles. This one, which I love. And another that's like a public smile, a "vote for me" smile, which I don't love.

I say, "Running Bird and I dreamwalked back to Lord Vertenomous's house. I heard him. He's there. And he's alive."

"He spoke to you?" she says, and sets down her pencil. I can tell she doesn't believe me. She can't shield well. I try to stay out of her mind, but sometimes it's hard.

"I heard him," I repeat stubbornly. "He sensed me, and he spoke. He called me Tex. No one else calls me that. It was Michael."

"Was Lindsey with him?"

"I don't know. I didn't hear her, but that doesn't mean she's not there, too."

"She never missed a chance to talk," Lauren says. "If she could have said something to you, she would have."

She sighs and starts tapping her pencil against her notepad. "So let me get this straight. You and Running Bird dreamwalked—or whatever it's called when you do it during the day, while you're awake—and wound up back at Lord Vertenomous's palace. Together. And you heard—but didn't see—someone who sounded like Michael, and now you're convinced he's alive?"

When I hear her say it that way, I have to admit that it does sound pretty crazy. I figure it's probably best if I leave out the parts about the Road Runner cartoon and traveling back in time.

"I know what I heard," I say. "And Running Bird heard it, too. He led me at first, but then I was leading. Look, I don't know where the talent comes from, but I was able to make us dreamwalk when we were awake. Running Bird was pretty surprised."

"So now he's convinced you're this Warrior Spirit, or you have it in you, or whatever?" she asks.

I'd been so distracted by thoughts of Michael that I'd forgotten that Running Bird asked me to sweat with him mostly to test me for Warrior Spirit possession.

"We didn't discuss it directly," I say.

Her eyebrows arch like the backs of angry cats. "Of course you didn't," she says, and sighs again. "Look, we can all talk this over later, you and Catlin and I. In the meantime, take this."

"What is it?"

"What you'll say at the meeting tonight. Memorize it if you can."

"Should I eat it after I'm finished?"

"What?"

"Like a secret message," I say weakly.

"This is serious," she says.

"What's it say?"

"It's just a convincing argument for why we should stay and fight. Don't worry," she says before I can interrupt. "It doesn't mention the smuggler or your dream. But we need to try to recruit members to SAF as soon as possible. Dylan has already been campaigning for the run-and-hide strategy. We have a lot of ground to make up."

"Captain of the debate team," I say, "weren't you?"

"It's a good thing I was," she says defensively.

So Lauren doesn't really believe Michael's alive, and Catlin might believe it but is angry with me because I want to do something about it. Neither response is exactly what I'd hoped for. But what if I'm wrong? About Michael. About everything. I'm frustrated and feeling lost. And going back to my tent to memorize my speech isn't going to fix anything.

I say, "Do you remember how, back when we were slaves at Lord Vertenomous's house, you once told me you wished you'd taken more time to just be?"

She looks suspicious. "Yeah. So?"

"So," I say, "let's go be."

At first she looks like she's going to resist, like she's organizing arguments that will attack my blasphemous "let's go be." But she surprises me, and maybe herself, too, by standing up.

"You know what? You're right." These aren't words I've heard very often from Lauren. I can't help enjoying them.

We take the main path up the mountain. After a long walk, some of it steep, both of us panting and sweating, we move above the tree line. Not long afterward, we come to a huge crater with a lake. We stop and catch our breath, then find a place to sit close to the water. The sun is more intense up here and reflects brightly off the white rocks. The air is warm.

"Feels like the top of the world," I say.

"It is beautiful," she says grudgingly, like she's admitting a rival has a good point. Lauren struggles with "just being." "Up here everything feels clean. Not like the lake I grew up by."

"Which lake is that?"

She frowns.

"That would be Lake Michigan," she says, a little more sarcastically than necessary, in my opinion.

"Oh, right."

Geography, when it comes to the Midwest, isn't my strong point. Lots of small square states.

"You *have* heard of the Great Lakes, right?" she asks. "Big lakes. No salt water."

"Of course," I say. "They're great."

"Used to be, maybe. Now they're gigantic cesspits, polluted by mills and refineries and exhaust and every kind of waste humans make. They say it isn't as bad as it used to be, but that's like saying somebody being poisoned isn't being given as much poison as they were before. They're still dying."

She is fighting a ghost war now. Her enemies, like her allies, are dead. Maybe, though, we can't give up on what we were even if what we were is mostly gone. So I listen to her talk about old causes. I listen until she pauses long enough for me to kiss her. She kisses me back. Then we're just a boy and a girl lying by a lake in the sun, kissing.

(((((14)))))

Something feels wrong. I don't know what it can be, and later I'll wonder if the feeling came before the alien ship showed up or after. But I do know the ship isn't directly above us when I feel it; the shadow of the ship moves over the bald stone top of the mountain just to the right of us. I can feel the probe, feel the alien in it searching.

"Stay very still," I say.

"It's close," Lauren says, a slight quiver to her voice, but that's all.

We're more out in the open than we should be. We shouldn't have left the protection of the trees. What was I thinking? I try to shield us both. Lauren tries to help, but the truth is she makes it harder when she tries to join with me: it pulls me away from what I'm trying to do.

"Don't," I say.

"I'm trying to help," she says.

"You aren't."

She pulls back. She's angry, but I can't worry about that right now. I have to hide us as much as I can. I try to make the reflection off the rocks more intense so that the alien won't see as well. I think thin, and I try to make us disappear in the light. I feel him looking and looking and maybe even for a second thinking he might see something, but he keeps going. He doesn't see us.

"That was close," I say.

"You should have let me help," she says.

"I'm sorry. I couldn't join for some reason."

Lie. It wasn't me who couldn't join. I think she knows it's a lie, but she doesn't call me on it.

"We should probably go back close to the tree line," I say.

"I've got some things to do anyway," she says.

"We can stay up here," I say. "Just, you know, at the tree line."

She shakes her head. "I really don't have time to be here right now. I'm sorry. Too many responsibilities."

"Like what?" I ask. The word *petulant*—another Mom vocabulary word—does sort of describe my voice.

It turns out she's volunteered to be Doc's secretary and organize his files, which she says are totally and outrageously disorganized. She's also organizing a group called New Bloods. She wants to start a dialogue between the New Bloods and the former house and clan members to facilitate New America. She expects my attendance. And, of course, there's SAF. That will take a lot of her time. This is her to-do list after just one day.

"We'll have time later," she says.

"Right," I say. "Another time."

We walk down the mountain. Here's the extent of our conversation. I slip on some loose rocks once, and she reminds me to be careful. She asks me for some water, and I pass her my water bottle.

We go our separate ways when we reach camp. We give each other a good-bye kiss, but she's rushing away in her mind before it's finished. Her lips bump awkwardly against mine, and she hurries off. Kind of reminds me of bumping into someone in the school hall. Something you'd mumble a quick "sorry" over before you moved on.

I can hear Michael's voice in my head: "Dude, which one of you is the girl?"

"Sexist," I'd say, sort of trying to sound like my mom. He'd laugh at me, and I'd laugh at me, too.

I walk back toward my tent, thinking I'll take a nap and try to stop thinking about things for a while. Lauren would definitely be disappointed at my slacker attitude. Fortunately, she'll be too busy to notice.

Unfortunately, there's a crowd of about twenty people at my tent. They're mostly sitting down in the grass like they've been there for a while.

"What's wrong?" I ask.

Some smart-buttocks says, "We've been invaded by aliens."

"Good one. I kind of meant something more specific."

"We're here to be trained. Doc told some people you were going to train us to fight like you do."

"Now?" I see my nap slipping off without me.

"You have something better to do?" a girl says.

Actually, yes, I think, but I say, "No."

My new students are in better shape than most new students to a program, but they're not in great shape. They need conditioning.

I get a question along these lines from several New Americans: "Why do we have to do all these exercises? We just want to learn how to fight."

I explain that being in good shape is necessary to being able to do the kicks and punches. I tell them that learning the physical moves is the first step. We'll try to work from the body to the mind.

Most of the students accept this with a minimum of grumbling, but a few walk away. They thought it would be easy, like learning how to make a sandwich. We always had people like that come to one or two martial-arts classes, too. They always quit.

Finally, at the end of a pretty grueling workout, when

everyone is exhausted, their clothes drenched in sweat, their faces streaked with dirt, I convert a physical move to a mental one. I try to show them how I do it, how I use a tae kwon do block to make a move in my mind that's like that tae kwon do block.

And fail. And try and fail. And try and fail. I don't know how to show or tell them.

I'm frustrated. They're frustrated. A woman named Cassandra takes pity on me and says, "You'll show us when you're able to show us."

I don't know if I'll ever be able to show them. I'm going to try, though. I'm going to keep trying.

«««((15)))»»»

When I get to the dinner area I see that Lauren, Catlin, Zack, and Zelda are all at a table. I get a tray and some food and walk over. As I'm sitting down, Catlin whispers she's sorry. A mind whisper. I tell her it's okay. And it is. Between us.

Zack tells me that everyone is talking about how I killed the alien patrol in Taos. We're sitting at one of the picnic tables back from the clearing, eating tortilla soup and bread. It's surprisingly good. If Michael were here, he'd be going back up and trying to talk the cooks into seconds.

Zack says, "Someone finally knows how to fight them. Finally."

"You're getting stronger," Catlin says to me, "aren't you? You're still getting stronger."

"I think so," I admit. "But that's normal, right?"

Normal? That word has lost its meaning.

"No," Catlin says. "People learn more about their talents, how to use them. This is different. Your talents are growing."

"Maybe it's not me," I say, smiling.

No one smiles back. Catlin, Zelda, and Zack look thoughtful. Lauren looks scornful.

"That was a joke," I say, but as often happens when you have to point out that you're joking, no one finds it any funnier than before.

Zack changes the subject. "I'm totally bummed I missed your training session today. I didn't know about it. Nobody told me."

"I didn't, either," I admit. I tell him I'm going to have one every afternoon now.

"I'll be there tomorrow," he promises. "I'll be an hour early."

"Just be on time, and you should be fine," I say. "I have a feeling there'll be plenty of room."

Zelda and Catlin say they'll come tomorrow, too.

Lauren frowns. "I'll come, too, of course," she says somewhat grudgingly. "But I'll have to rearrange my afternoon. You should have told me before you set the time. We should make a schedule of events."

Catlin changes the subject: "Zelda was just telling

us she has more than one talent," she says. "It's rare to have more than one."

Zelda looks at me shyly. "I'm a good listener. You already know that. My strongest talent, though, is forecasting the weather. I can tell you, with a hundred percent accuracy, what the weather will be tomorrow. I mean, where I am, not everywhere. Tomorrow it's going to be sunny, no rain, high eighty-one, low forty-nine, by the way."

"So you're like Storm from *X-Men*," Lauren says. I think she says this for my sake, maybe to prove that we have movies in common, too. I appreciate the effort, even if she's a little confused about the details.

"I wish I could control the weather like Storm," Zelda says. "I'm more like a totally awesome meteorologist."

"My talent is going to be fighting," Zack says again, as though saying it enough times will make it so.

"The gods will decide," Zelda says. "You shouldn't really talk about it."

Doc comes up to our table and asks us how we're doing and how the food is. We all say it's good. It almost feels like I'm back in school and the principal is visiting our table. Every once in a while my old life pushes into my new one, but it feels more and more like a stranger.

Doc asks me how the training went. He heard I worked everyone pretty hard. I admit that I did. Then I tell him how I'm struggling to show people how to fight like I do.

"Just teach people martial arts," he says. "The rest will come."

"I'll try," I say. "I'm not really a teacher."

"Everyone is a student and a teacher," he says.

Spoken like a teacher.

But that doesn't mean it's not true.

(((((16)))))

I tell the others I'll see them at the meeting. I head to the Porta-Potties. Whoever came up with that name for plastic outdoor toilets must be, like, three years old. There are six in a row downstream from the main camp. Sometimes there's a line, but I'm in luck today and don't have to wait.

When I step out, someone is waiting. She's leaning against a tree with her arms folded.

"So you talked to Doc about having me train a bunch of pilots for this suicide mission of yours. Thanks so much," Sam says.

"I wouldn't say I talked to him, exactly," I say, unable to gauge how she feels about it.

We start walking toward the town meeting, joining others who are heading that way.

"Doesn't matter," she says. "I'm ready as long as we have the right leader."

"And who would that be?"

"The obvious choice is me."

"I wouldn't say 'obvious.'"

"Former sergeant in the Rangers. Elite soldier. Me."

"I'm the one with the Warrior Spirit."

"I thought you didn't believe in that nonsense."

"I'm coming around. Anyway, it's my idea."

"An idea that you have no idea how to execute. Have you ever led a mission? I've led many, *and* I've been in combat situations. You've been in high school."

She has a point.

"Okay," I say, and I smile a little because I know I've got her. "Fine. You lead if it means so much to you."

We're at a narrow part of the path, and she shoves me off it. I have to catch myself on a branch.

"You're kind of childish for a combat leader," I say.

"You're kind of annoying for a Chosen One. And you need to work on your balance."

"You can call me Jesse. You don't think I'm a god anyway."

"Not even half," she says. "So, *Jesse,* any bright ideas on where I'm going to find these potential pilots we're going to need? You don't usually get a lot of volunteers for suicide missions."

"It's not a suicide mission. And I already know of one other pilot: Catlin."

I know I shouldn't put Catlin in danger, but I want her along. We've fought together before. Anyway, she's a healer, a good one. We might need her.

"Okay," she says. "What about your other girlfriend?"

"I only have one girlfriend. Lauren is my girlfriend."

"Really?" she says.

"Really."

"If you say so," she says.

"Anyway," I say, "Lauren wouldn't be good for this."

"Why not?"

"Lauren isn't talented. Or she has a little talent but not much." Saying this feels like a betrayal. But not saying it would be wrong, too.

"Oh," she says. "Okay. No Lauren."

"We can probably take only six people total anyway," I say. "Three is a full ship. They should all be pilots, right? Except me."

"That's why I'm the planner," Sam says. "We'll have a truck drive out with a unit. Maybe ten or so soldiers. They can leave just before dark and be there before it's light. They can fly back with us. We'll be a squadron then."

"That's actually a good idea," I admit.

We reach the town meeting, which is packed with people. I'm shielding the cacophony of voices without even realizing it. I search the crowd for Lauren's face, or Catlin's.

You really think this can make a difference? Sam mindspeaks. *Stealing ships. Blowing them up.*

"I don't know," I admit.

She rolls her eyes. Then, as if she's been testing me and I've just failed, she says, "Try to be a little more positive with the recruits, okay?"

"Yeah," I say.

"Anyway," she says, "what's the worst that could happen? The aliens get angry and want to kill us." She laughs.

"I suppose the worst would be we all die during the raid," I can't help pointing out.

"Another thing you shouldn't say to the recruits," she says.

I look over the crowd again for Lauren, but I don't see her. I see Catlin talking to Zelda and Zack. I watch her for a few seconds, then look away.

"Why did you say 'oh' like that when I said Lauren doesn't have much talent?" I ask Sam.

No answer. I turn. No Sam.

(((((17)))))

The town meeting is almost as well attended as the one last night. It's at the same time, so the sun has already slipped behind the mountains and the day has slipped away with it. Running Bird and Doc are at the front again. I walk over to where Catlin and the others are.

"I've saved a seat for you," Zack says a bit louder than necessary, like he hopes other people will overhear. He acts like I'm a celebrity. And he's not the only one. I can feel other people looking at me the same way Zack does. But none of them are seeing me. They're seeing something they hope I am.

Doc announces news of New America. He kind of makes a point of calling it that. Mary Sanchez had her baby. The community garden is going well. The search parties charged with looking for farm animals have good news: two roosters have been found.

"We don't need the boys," a woman says. "We need the girls. We need some huevos rancheros."

Laughter. You'd think no one would be able to laugh anymore, but you'd be wrong. People find ways. It's one of the things about people that is a good surprise.

Doc promises that we'll have hens before the end of the month. I can't help thinking that we may not be here—or anywhere—by the end of the month. These thoughts are never far away, though I'm glad I'm at least able to shield them now. I guess they exist side by side with the laughter here at the end of the world.

Then it's time for open discussion. The woman whose tent is next to the snorer is first, and she gets pretty worked up about the need for a good night's sleep and how the roosters will just make this harder.

"We already have the loudest snorer in the world," she says. "Something needs to be done."

The snorer follows her and offers a rebuttal. He talks about freedom and individual rights. He considers his tent his property, and he believes his right to snore in his tent is protected under the Constitution. I'm not all that familiar with the Constitution, but I'm pretty sure there's no right-to-snore amendment. The snorer ends by saying, "Give me liberty or give me death," which isn't the smartest thing in the world to say to a woman who looks like the choice would be an easy one for her.

Then Lauren has her turn. She stands and says that

the snorer's comments have made her think that we, in New America, should consider a new constitution. Then she tells the rebels about SAF and the New Bloods Club, and she says I will explain some reasons why SAF is so important.

Because of my training session this afternoon, I didn't have time to memorize the script Lauren gave me. But I don't need a script to know why I think staying and fighting is the best — the *only* — option. "Look," I say, "I know that running away sounds tempting. But do you really think there's anywhere we could hide where the aliens wouldn't find us eventually? We all know how powerful they are. To be honest, we may die no matter what we do. I'd rather die fighting." I sit down. There's an uncomfortable silence.

Lauren's eyes remind me of one of my favorite old martial-arts movies, *Daggers of Death*. I can hear her thinking how I'm totally messing up the presentation and how I should have stuck to the script.

Dylan jumps up on the stage and looks out over the crowd as if it's assembled just to come and hear him speak. "The New Blood is wrong. We don't have to die. Make me your leader, and I will lead you to safety."

Lauren jumps up on the stage, too. It's getting kind of crowded up there. Just before she says what she's about to say, I hear her say it in my mind. I consider rushing the stage to stop her, but I don't. Maybe it's right that everyone should know. Maybe Lauren's right. She says, "Dylan is wrong. There are more aliens coming. Millions more. My friends and I met an alien smuggler who told us this, and Jesse had a dream and saw them. Millions. They're a few weeks away, but they're coming."

There's an explosion of voices, both mindspeak and vocal. "Millions?" *Millions?* They're frightened and angry, and the sharpness of their feelings gives the air a quiver.

"All the more reason for us to find a safe place now!" Dylan shouts above the noise. "We can't fight millions."

People are asking Doc if this is true, if there are millions more aliens coming.

"What is true," he says, "is that the newcomers have been told by an alien that more aliens are coming. What is true is that Jesse had a dream that seemed to support this statement. But other than the dream and the word of an alien, we have no verification of this information. Can we rely on the word of an alien?"

It's the first time I've seen the politician Doc. He's good.

"But if he's right," someone says, "and millions more are coming, then what do we do?"

There's the pop of nerves everywhere, anxiety crackling in the air. *What do we do? What do we do?*

Dylan says, "It doesn't matter if they're coming or not. Enough are here that we can't stay. We know we're being hunted. We stay here, and we die. I say we live. We hide. We survive. We keep alive so that one day our sons and daughters may fight."

"We can't," I whisper.

Desperation ripples through the crowd, and not even my strongest shield can protect me from the sheer force of it. So then I try to tell them what I told Doc and Running Bird about the possibility of the settlers not settling here. I try to say this is our chance. We've got to stop them somehow.

They listen, but they're too afraid to see this as hopeful. I can't really blame them.

"*That's* our best shot?" a strangled voice calls.

We need to run and hide! A lot of people are mind-speaking this. *Run and hide.*

Running Bird calls all the minds to him, and they obey. His voice is so loud that it's hard not to. It's weird: sometimes Running Bird seems like a total joke, and sometimes he seems like the most powerful person in New America. "The Chosen One is saying that the first way and the second way, the fighting and the running, will not save us. He's saying there is a third way."

I am? I thought I was saying we were screwed either way—more or less. Better to fight and probably die than run and probably die was what I thought I was saying.

Running Bird mindspeaks just to me. *Keep quiet, Warrior Boy.*

The third way catches on immediately with the crowd. It's a big hit. I can feel the anger and confusion take on a different hue. The Warrior Spirit is leading the Chosen One with a third way. This is just the kind of thing the Warrior Spirit would do. Yes.

There's no third way, I mindspeak to Running Bird.

Maybe you don't know what you know. Maybe the Spirit hasn't revealed it to you yet.

Maybe I don't know what I know, but I know what I *don't* know, and I don't know a third way. Still, I keep quiet.

"What is the third way?" someone asks.

"He cannot tell us yet," Running Bird says. "The Spirit is not ready for him to reveal all."

You'd think people would see right through this and call him on it. But they don't. They want to believe. They need to.

Someone prays that the Chosen One gets the information soon before more are killed. I hear amens all over the crowd.

A lot of people look at me with hope. Lauren and Dylan look displeased—or, more accurately, disgusted.

My eyes seek out Catlin. She alone looks at me with sympathy. Only Catlin seems to know how I feel without my saying a word.

18

As soon as the meeting is adjourned, I rush off into the dark to get away from all those voices. All that want and need. No matter what Running Bird says, I can't save these people.

But there's one person I *can* save. I've been going back and forth and back and forth about it. Is this the choice that the man at the circus foresaw or remembered or whatever? Do I take the chance that Michael — irritating ex-jock, fellow former slave, best friend Michael — is really alive and try to save him, or do I do the smart and safe thing and stay where I am? Is this the choice?

I hide out in my tent for a few hours, ignoring the gentle "knocks" and whispers from people wanting to talk to me, including Lauren and Zack, until the camp is quiet. I wait until they're all tucked away in their tents. Slowly, I unzip my tent flap and crawl outside. The air is chilly. I reach back inside to get a jacket.

"Where do you think you're going?" Lauren says. I didn't hear her unzipping her tent, but there she stands.

Just then, Catlin comes up the trail. She looks beautiful in the moonlight—both of them look beautiful. It's an odd thought for that particular moment, but what can I say? Sometimes a girl in the moonlight or girls in the moonlight will trump everything.

Catlin doesn't look startled to see us, and I'm happy to see her because now I won't have to find her.

"I'm going to go get Michael," I tell Lauren.

"No, you aren't," Lauren says. "You can't."

"Actually, I can."

"We're hanging on by a thread here. You can't be so selfish."

"He's my best friend. If there's even a chance he's alive, I've got to go. Maybe I'm even supposed to go."

"First of all," Lauren says, "that's total crap. You're supposed to be here helping us organize this group. Anyway, you can't even be sure it was him. It was just a dream. Or maybe some kind of hypnotic trance Running Bird forced on you. Second, you remember how long it took to drive here? You'd be gone half a week even if you managed to get there and back, which is unlikely. Third, these people are counting on you. SAF is counting on you. We have to focus on that."

"I'm not going to drive to Austin," I say.

This stops Lauren, who, I think, is about to launch into an even longer explanation of what I can and can't do.

Catlin smiles. "You were coming to get me, weren't you? You need me to fly you."

"Maybe," I say.

Lauren frowns at both of us. "Those ships belong to New America."

"Technically, I helped steal the one today," I say. "I think I'm entitled to one night's use. We can be back by morning."

"You can't do this."

"It's Michael we're talking about," I say. "We can't leave him."

"Michael is just one person. You have to think about everyone here now. They look to you for leadership. I can help. I can help you lead them. We'll do it together. But first you have to see that you have a responsibility to the whole group. One person is just one person, no matter who he or she is."

Maybe I'm not suited to leadership, because one person is not just one person to me. Michael is not just another person.

I can see what Lauren's about to do. I have an image of it, like I've stepped a few moments into the future. In that future, she screams. She wakes up the camp to prevent me from leaving. Or she will.

I don't have time to wonder how I manage to step ahead in time, or if it's even possible to prevent something that's already happened — already written in the book, Running Bird would say. I just react.

"I'm sorry," I say.

"For what?" Lauren says.

I'm as gentle as I can be, but I do it fast. I put her to sleep. I'm not even sure I can do it until I do. I rush to catch her and end up mostly breaking her fall by letting her fall on top of me.

So if all is/was/will be written in the Big Book of Time or the Universe or whatever, then how did I change what was written? Unless it was written that I would change what was written. Confusing. Not so confusing is that Lauren is a heavy body of unconscious flesh fallen on top of me.

"A little help," I say.

Catlin helps me move Lauren. We get her back in her tent and into her sleeping bag. When we're outside again, I ask, "So are you going with me?"

"Are you going to make me go to sleep if I say no?"

I shake my head. "You wouldn't tell," I say. "You

might not go with me. You might tell me I was being a fool, but you wouldn't start screaming."

"She's not wrong, you know," Catlin says. "You are being a fool, but I guess I'm a fool, too."

"So we'll be fools together," I say.

We start down the mountain on the wide path to the cars. The stars are bright in the sky. Billions. Trillions. They make me feel small and large at the same time.

We're at the edge of camp, down by the plastic Porta-Potties, when we run into Zack. We don't see him in time, and he reads us.

"I'm coming along," he says.

"No, you're not," I say.

"Then I'm going to start screaming and tell them what you plan to do. You can't stop me."

I can, I think. He thinks right back, *Not in time.* He's stronger than Lauren. He could be right. Maybe I can't stop him in time.

"Look," I say, "it's dangerous. There's no reason for you to come. You don't even know him."

"I knew the others."

"What others?" Catlin says.

"All the others they took or killed," he says. "My parents. My friends."

Catlin says, "It's too dangerous, Zack."

"If I can get one person back . . ." Zack says. His voice breaks. I hear him curse in his mind. "If I can get one person back, it will make a difference."

How can I say no to him, even knowing how dangerous it is? We all have little holes in our hearts, and we all would give anything to fill even just one of them.

"Please," he says. "I need to do something. I need to take something from them."

I do a stupid thing then. I nod yes. "But you have to do exactly what I say," I add.

"I will."

Catlin mindspeaks to me, *Are you sure about this?*

Not at all, I mindspeak back.

I turn to Zack, already regretting my decision. "You'll do what I say? No questions?"

"Whatever you tell me," he promises.

As we walk down the mountain, the dark of the night in the trees, the silence all around us, I think about Michael and those first days after the invasion.

Michael and I didn't like each other at first. He'd been a football star in high school, and he had a big ego. So there was that. Also, when we were enslaved, he acted like it was all worse for him because he was African-American and his ancestors had been slaves. Maybe it was, but it was so bad for everyone I didn't think we should be measuring our sorrows against each other.

We'd all lost everyone, or almost everyone, we'd loved. We'd all lost everything we were. We'd all become someone's property.

We nearly got in a fight. But somehow we got past all that and became friends. He called me Tex because he was from Florida and I was from Texas. He called me a lot of other things, too, not all of them nice. It's hard to explain. We were really different, but there was some way we were also really alike.

One night, when we were lying on our blankets about to go to sleep, I told him that I thought of him like a brother. It was a weak moment, I'll grant you. His response? "We aren't frickin' girls."

"Hence the term *brothers*," I said. "If we were girls, we would be sisters."

Michael as a girl—that made me laugh. He would be about the ugliest girl ever.

"Look," he said, "we're cool. We don't have to get all touchy-feely."

"I love you, man." I put out my arms to hug him. He recoiled. It was so easy to annoy him, and I really enjoyed it.

"You are annoying," he said.

"Brotherly love," I said. "We all need brotherly love."

"Yeah," he said. "A white guy from Texas is my brother. As my mother used to say, what is the world coming to?"

"Good question," I said, because there was no good answer to that one.

Lauren will understand why I had to do what I had to do when I get him back. She'll see Michael, and she'll realize she was wrong and forgive me. I tell myself this. Unfortunately, I answer myself, too. *Lauren won't understand. And she definitely won't forgive you. You are an idiot if you think she will.*

This is a good example of why people who talk to themselves should never answer themselves.

19

It takes us about ten minutes to get down the mountain to the cars and trucks and motorcycles and then another fifteen to drive down the windy road to the big red barn where the ships are kept. When we park, I look back up the mountain and think of all those people asleep, of Lauren in her tent. I'm betraying them all.

"This is going to be so awesome," Zack says. "We're going to kick some alien butt!"

"Right," I say.

"Should I call you the Chosen One?" he asks. "I mean, is it okay if I do?"

"No."

"But maybe they've heard of you. Him. The story of him in you, I mean. Maybe it will scare the aliens."

I look at Zack and see the way he bites his lip, and I see how frightened he is. I could put him to sleep here. I consider it but decide that he deserves to make his own choice. We all deserve that.

"Go ahead if you want," I say, because I can tell that Zack really needs this. "Just on the mission, though. Not after."

"Okay, Chosen One!" Zack says.

Catlin catches my eye and gives me her soft half smile. She doesn't need to mindspeak to me for me to know that she approves.

We climb aboard the newer ship, the one Sam flew back from Taos this morning. Zack gets in first and takes shotgun, and I have to tell him to get in the back. He gives me a petulant look but does what I say. Catlin gets the ship up and going quickly.

"This one is faster," she says.

"Faster than the others?"

Her hand presses more firmly into the hand control. The ship jerks forward.

"See? Faster."

"That's good, right?" I say. "We'll get there sooner."

"I guess," she says. But I can tell she's not entirely comfortable with this new ship. Or maybe with the idea of getting back to Lord Vertenomous's palace faster.

"Go higher," I say.

It's a clear night. The aliens don't like heights. My thinking is if we're high, we'll probably be above them. Up here I can almost imagine that the world isn't completely changed down there. And in a way I guess it isn't. We were the rulers of the planet just a year ago. We aren't anymore, but the planet doesn't know it. The planet doesn't miss us. What's not the same is us. Like other species that were once the rulers of the world, our time is over.

Except that I won't accept that. I can't.

The Hunter waits for me. He's not going to just give me Michael and wish me a nice day. I have a feeling he knows I'm coming. I have a feeling he has planned a welcome that isn't particularly welcoming.

"Maybe I should go low and slow," she says nervously. "Low and slow is good."

"We have a better chance of not being caught high and fast."

"Wait," she says, as though she's listening to something else. She's interacting with the ship. She says she's found some presets in the control panel. She picks one.

We go higher. It's kind of like when you're in a plane; it's hard to tell just how fast we're moving from so high. Fast, though, I think. In just a couple of hours we're in the hill country west of Austin. It's still dark, still night, but the moon hangs in the same place in the sky and casts its somber blue light over the hills.

When we get close, Catlin says, "Now what?"

"Slow down," I say, "and maybe fly a bit lower so we can see where we are."

We pass over Lake Travis and a fat cement dam and down what becomes a river again below it. I'm pretty sure I can see Lord Vertenomous's palace on one of the hills to the east. The rich person who built the palace actually chopped off the top of a hill so he'd have space for his pools and gardens. He must have had a ridiculous amount of money. Doesn't matter now, of course. He could have been the richest person in the world, and it wouldn't matter now.

We follow the river. Cliffs rise along the north side. Then the land flattens out, and a grassy park spreads back from the shore. I remember coming to this park one Easter with my uncle and dad and mom. City Park. We grilled fajitas and went up and down the lake in my uncle's boat.

"Let's land down there," I say, nodding toward the park.

"Why? I can land us a few hundred yards away from the palace. Isn't it a good idea to have the ship close? They will be trying to, you know, kill us."

You don't have to be the Chosen One to know that. But I'm worried they'll have some way of detecting an incoming ship. They won't expect a car, which I'm hoping to find at one of the houses just up from the park. We argue this point. Either way might be right. Either way might be wrong.

"I vote to land in the park," Zack says.

Catlin says he's just trying to get in good with the Warrior Spirit, but she steers the ship over to the park and makes a perfect landing.

"You're getting good at that," I say.

"Obvious flattery because you got your way," she says, "but I'll take it."

We start walking up the hill. It's hotter here in Austin than in the mountains around Taos. It's quieter, too. No insects or other animals here. The only sounds are our sounds: our breathing, our shoes on the black-top road.

Being back here in Austin, walking past the empty houses, reminds me of a conversation I had one time with this friend of mine from high school, Kevin Wayne. We were talking about the end of the world. Not because the aliens had just landed or anything like that. No, this was back when the end of the world was impossible. It was back when the thought of it was a game.

We were sitting on the front steps of our high school on a lazy spring afternoon.

Kevin said, "What would you do today if you knew the world was going to end tomorrow?"

"I don't know," I said. It seemed like one of those ridiculous questions a teacher asks to get a class talking. It was impossible to imagine.

He offered me a cigarette. Though Kevin was a

wrestler, he was also a smoker. He claimed they offset each other. I declined, as always, which didn't stop him from asking every day.

"I know what I'd do," he said. "I would go to the Save Yourself for Marriage Girls and say, 'Listen up, girls. It's no use. There's no time for marriage. I will help you experience carnal pleasures in these, our last hours. I'll give myself to you.'"

Kevin was obsessed with the Save Yourself for Marriage Girls—or the hot ones, anyway. He called them misguided. He was always saying he wanted to help them go beyond their limitations. I wasn't totally surprised that he thought he'd spend the last hours of his life with the Save Yourself for Marriage Girls.

But I know now that he was wrong. He would not spend his last hours with people he didn't know. He'd spend them with people he cared about, people he loved.

You don't realize how much the people you love matter until you don't have them. How stupid is that? I wasted so much time before the invasion. If I'd just paid more attention, if I'd just lived the day I was in instead of always thinking of the day I hadn't gotten to yet . . . It seems so obvious now, but I never quite believed it.

"Look over there," Catlin says, pulling me out of the memory.

She points at a driveway with a car in it. As I hoped,

the demolition crews haven't made it out here yet. If they had, every car would be destroyed.

"Let's see if we can find the keys," I say.

Fortunately, the front door of the house is unlocked. We go in. It's one of those big stucco houses with high ceilings and tall windows.

As soon as we step from the entryway into the living room, the smell hits us.

"Gods," Zack says, his hand covering his mouth as he gags.

Two bodies are lying on the floor, just visible in the moonlight.

"They missed a couple," Catlin says.

After the invasion, the aliens collected the bodies: people, animals, everything that was once alive that they'd put to sleep—permanent sleep, it turned out. All those bodies scattered everywhere were gone in days. We don't know where or how they were taken, but the aliens cleaned things up with super speed.

"I'm sorry I said that," Catlin says. "You see so many people die, and you start getting used to it. That's not right."

We spread out and search for the keys, which takes longer than we'd like because of how dark it is. Just as I'm starting to think that maybe we'd be better off searching another house—one without bodies rotting in the next room—Catlin finds a bunch of keys in a bowl on the kitchen counter. She grabs them all, and we hurry outside, careful not to look at the decaying bodies again.

The first set of keys doesn't work, and I toss them into the bushes. The next set does. I get in the driver's seat, and Catlin, complaining that she knows how to drive, has her learner's permit anyway, and needs practice, reluctantly gets in the passenger side. Zack gets in back again.

I try to drive in the dark without the lights at first, but the road winds through the hills and there's a steep drop off the gravel shoulder in places. Catlin says we should join to do a cloaking.

"I've never joined," Zack says.

"Just watch this time," I say, remembering how Lauren's clumsy efforts made joining impossible.

Catlin and I join as easily as holding hands. And there's something else: our cloak is stronger than before. I can feel that we're completely hidden.

"Awesome," Zack says.

I even turn the headlights on, which is a good thing since I wasn't really seeing where we were going. We've taken a wrong turn and have to backtrack. Fortunately, Lord Vertenomous's house isn't far, and even with the backtracking, we're there in just a few minutes.

We park close to the gate. I'm still joined with Catlin, and I feel her begin to shake; it's like a shiver runs through our joining. I think of one of my mom's sayings: "Ghost walked over your grave."

I never really understood that saying before. How could a ghost walk over my grave? I didn't have a grave — not yet. Of course, if Running Bird is right, I *do* have a grave, just in another moment. Which means that someone could walk over it. I could shiver.

I pull away from Catlin. It's an odd feeling, almost like pulling away from an embrace and missing the other person's warmth.

"It's going to be okay," I say to cover my awkwardness and reassure all three of us. But I'm not sure even I believe me.

I pull the car off the road and into a copse of trees. We get out and walk toward the stone wall that encircles the palace, trying our best to be as silent and as invisible as possible, though we've yet to catch sight of an alien ship or guard. Everything is still and quiet. Too still. Too quiet.

There's an iron gate blocking the entry at the top of the drive and a guardhouse just beyond the gate. I don't know if anyone's in the guardhouse — it's too dark to see — but we won't be going in that way. Too risky. We circle around the wall. It's about seven or eight feet tall, impossible to see over.

"I don't feel any sensors, do you?" I ask in a whisper.

Neither Catlin nor Zack feels anything. But instead of making me feel more comfortable, it worries me. It's too easy.

"I'll give you a boost," I say to Catlin. "You check it out. If it's okay, go over."

"How am I going to go over?" She's small, about five one. She says she's five one, anyway, but it's possible she's rounding up.

"Hang from the wall and drop," I say.

"Oh, is that all?" she says sarcastically.

"Let me go first," Zack says.

I hesitate, but he *is* a little taller than Catlin. And he doesn't seem intimidated by the thought of an eight-foot drop. We boost him up to the wall. He balances there for a bit and looks around. Then he shrugs and disappears over the other side.

I boost Catlin up and hear Zack coaxing her to jump, promising to catch her. I can't blame her for having her doubts about that. I manage to find a toehold and quickly scramble up about the same time as Catlin lands on Zack and they both tumble to the ground. I drop down next to them.

"This place is unreal," Zack whispers, sitting up and looking around at the grounds and the big white palace beyond them.

"I need to get in better shape," Catlin says, rubbing her shoulder.

"When we get back, I can help you get in shape," I say.

"Yeah," Zack says. "You can join our training group."

When we get back. I'm using the power of positive thinking here. My power of positive thinking isn't very powerful, though.

"Keep looking for traps," I say to them as I start walking toward the house.

I don't feel any, though. And we don't see any guards, either, but we do see ships. There must be hundreds of them parked in the giant lot where the ships were parked before we escaped. It worries me that there's no security. It seems too easy.

We get all the way up to the house before Catlin says, "Wait."

Zack and I stop, and Zack even crouches a little like he expects to be hit.

"There's a spell on the doors," she says.

"They aren't really spells, you know," I say. She's the only one who calls them that. She's the only one I've met who thinks of this power of the mind as magical. It's us. It's not magic. She thinks it is.

"Whatever you want to call it, this door is booby-trapped."

Finally I get an image of the "spell" Catlin is talking about. But I get an image of something else from Catlin, too, one that floats in her mind for a second.

"Were you a member of the Harry Potter fan club when you were younger?" I say. "Because I'm pretty sure I just saw some kind of club symbol."

"Stay out of my mind," she orders.

" 'Harry Potter Rules'? Was that your motto?"

Zack laughs. She glares at him and tells me to shut up.

"You were president of the club, weren't you?"

She shoves me a little. "They're great books."

"Sure," I say, "but a fan club?"

"I was eight, okay? Can we just, you know, get on with saving Michael and escaping the aliens and getting home in one piece?"

Home. The weird thing is, I feel that way, too. The rebel camp is kind of home. New America is kind of home.

I look at the door, but whatever is protecting it is complicated. Too complicated for me.

"We should join," I say.

She agrees, and we open ourselves to each other. Our minds pull together. A word comes to me that I don't want: *intimate.* Joining with Catlin is intimate. It's my mom's word. It makes me uncomfortable that I'm so comfortable with her.

We feel our way to the door and undo the alarm first and then the block on it. We're careful. We work together. We are together, almost like one. We're so close that when we finish and step through the door and break our joining, I feel lost for a moment.

"I've never seen anyone join like you guys join," Zack whispers. "People always said my mom and dad were good at joining, but they were nothing like you two. You make it look easy."

I can't meet Catlin's eyes. It's almost like we've been caught kissing or something, even though joining isn't anything like kissing. It's just about increasing our power. That's all.

Lord Vertenomous's palace feels different from when we lived here. The house isn't full of minds. When I was a slave here, there were sixty of us plus Handlers and the staff. But now all of the humans are gone. A few of us escaped, but most were killed. I can feel that, feel the horrible truth of it, and I'm pretty sure Catlin and Zack can, too.

We pass through the room where we ate and had an hour to relax in the evenings. The room where Betty died. It looks different. The tables have been taken out. It looks more like a big living room. I can feel a spike of fear in Catlin. I know she's thinking about Lord Vertenomous.

He's dead, I mindspeak. *You're safe. Safe from him, anyway.*

Way to be reassuring, she mindspeaks back.

I have the touch.

"There's something really strong here," Zack says. "Really strong."

Catlin frowns. "I don't hear anything. Not even Michael."

I force myself to reach out around us, to listen more intently. I check the rooms upstairs and hear the aliens in their beds, but I know almost immediately that the Hunter isn't up there.

I broaden my search from the upstairs to the first floor, to the back. I don't hear the Hunter, but I do hear a voice, a human voice. Michael's. It's faint; he's dreaming. That's when I realize he isn't in the house; he's below it. In something like a basement, maybe. The word *dungeon* comes to mind.

"The library," I say, following Michael's dream until I'm as close to the source as I can get from up here. Michael's dream comes from under the room filled with books.

"There's a way down," I say. "It's in here somewhere."

"Down where?" Zack says.

"The basement," I say. *Dungeon,* I think.

"I don't see a door," Catlin says.

And then I can see what Catlin and I think of at the same time. "Secret passage," I say.

"It must be behind the books," she says.

We pull out books as quickly and quietly as possible. Then I see it. It's a button that's the color of the stain on the shelves. I push it, and the shelves slide back.

"Awesome," Zack says.

"The guy had too much money," I say, trying to sound like Lauren. The truth? It *is* awesome.

We're all about to go down, but then I have an important thought: one way in probably means one way out.

"You two stay here," I say. "I'll get him."

"It makes more sense for you to stay here," Catlin says. "You can fight them better than we can. No one is down there guarding him."

I scan the cell and see that she's right. She's right most of the time. But she's quiet about it. A lot of people probably don't even notice how right she is most of the time.

"Okay," I say. "You two go. I'll just wait here. Maybe read a book."

They rush down the stairs. I locate Michael's voice and call his name as loudly as I can.

"Wake up, Sleeping Beauty," I say.

He mumbles a little about steak and potatoes and rolls over.

An excellent plan, but with at least one or two fatal flaws, a voice says.

My body tenses. My breath quickens. *Fatal* is definitely not a word I want to hear right now. FLIGHT. FLIGHT. My whole body yearns for this choice. But I know it's not really an option.

FIGHT.

(((((20)))))

A shiver runs through my body as I look for him. I see myself in a grave. For a moment it feels like I've walked into the future again. It's set. It will happen. But then I remember how I could put Lauren to sleep even after I saw her waking the camp. I changed the future.

I can change the future.

The Hunter, *hunters,* appear. I was fearing one, but now I see a dozen. A dozen dealers of death — my death. Sandpaper throat. Wobbly legs. It takes all my will to face them.

Think, I think. It's always a bad sign when you have to tell yourself to think, when you have to hope that the word will actually remind you to do something you should already be doing.

I look at the many hunters, and I realize that something is wrong — I mean, besides the obvious wrong place/wrong time. He's smiling—*they're* smiling—in exactly the same way. In fact, they look exactly the same.

My terrified little brain finally kicks into gear, and I start forcing the hunters to fade away until I come to the real one, which doesn't fade but glows stronger in the darkness.

You see right through me, don't you? You see the real me. None of my wives have been able to see the real me. I blame it on the modern Empire.

I will say this for this Hunter: he has a good time—I mean, in a homicidal alien maniac kind of way.

"I don't want any trouble," I say. "Let us go, and I won't kill you."

Trash talk. Well, polite trash talk with a definite wishful component.

I can't do that, so I guess you'll just have to go ahead and kill me, product.

Still smiling. He's so confident in his strength and my weakness he doesn't even bother to create a strong shield. I'm an ant to him. He will squash me when he's done playing with me.

"I'd rather not," I say. This is actually true. I don't want to kill him even in the very unlikely event that I could. "Come on, let us go. Just this once. It will make the whole hunting experience more fun for you."

He snaps his fingers, and a document of some kind appears in his hand. How, I don't know. The mind can't make something appear from nothing. Magic. I make a mental note not to tell Catlin about this.

I don't think our contract has a provision where I let you go. He looks it over in a dramatic, overacted kind of way. So maybe he is a hundred times stronger than me, but he's no Johnny Depp when it comes to acting. *No, nothing in here about predator letting prey go. Sorry, afraid you have to die.* He tosses the document in the air, and it disappears.

I frantically look for a weakness in him. Anything. Anything. Nothing.

I do have a weakness, he mindspeaks. *I have a weakness for games. Here's a clue. I have one great passion. I'll give you five seconds to guess what it is. Four, three . . .*

I'm not much of a game person, but this seems like a good time to make an exception.

Two—

"Um," I say, "hunting?"

And they say your species is stupid. I never thought so. I've hunted all manner of creatures, you know. The great ones like the serpents of Radian Eight, eight-headed creatures able to shoot poison from any of those heads from fifty feet. Massive bodies. They can only be killed when the central head—and there is really no way to know which head that is until you find it—is chopped off. And I've hunted the weak, too. Even weaker than your species. Does the fact that I love killing make me a bad Sanginian? I don't think so.

"I do," I say.

We are all predator and prey. It is as natural to the universe as gravity. Naturally, prey is bound to feel there is a certain unfairness inherit in the relationship.

Except we're not supposed to be prey, I mindspeak at him. *We're not product, and you know it.*

I want you to know that I intend to mount your head on my wall with my other trophy heads. Dreamwalking is rare, and I like the cheeky way you escaped me.

"I'm sure it's an honor," I say, "but I'd rather keep my head."

Maybe I can convince you otherwise.

The lights come on, greenish rather than the familiar yellow tone, and I see other aliens enter the room. Two from the front and another from the back. They're all small, with big power. Not as big as the Hunter's, but big.

"Crap," I say, too frazzled to be more inventive with my language — sorry, Mom. I try to send a warning to Catlin and Zack. I'm not sure it gets through, though. The glow of the Hunter's power feels like it's all around me, encircling me, smothering me.

Here's an interesting question. Does product-that-is-not-product who dies where no one can see it ever really exist? My employers would say no. Def-in-ite-ly no. The product-that-is-not-product never existed.

"I'd like to debate that point," I say. "In public."

I would want Lauren right there beside me. She would kick the alien's butt in a debate. He'd be all, "A hunter should hunt." And she would give him like a million reasons why he was wrong in general and especially wrong when he was talking about humans.

If you give us the location of the product you've been hiding with, I might give you another minute or two of life. Most prey will give anything for an extra minute or two. Most of their lives have passed unnoticed by them. Minutes, hours, days, weeks, entire years in your way of measuring time. But for two minutes they will do anything. How about you?

"Can I think about it?" Some people are good at stalling, and some are not. Guess which kind I am?

Just then, Catlin, Zack, and Michael slip out from behind the bookcase. It's a relief to see Michael. He's real. He's alive. He looks worn and thin, and he's limping, but he has that unmistakable mischievous twinkle to his dark eyes. He would hate to hear me think *twinkle*. I make a note to say it to him — several times — in the unlikely event we survive.

"Damn, Tex," he says. "You didn't have to wake the whole house, did you?"

Zack tries to laugh, but it comes out like a squawk. His face is pale, and the skin around his small mouth is stretched tight. I'm worried he'll faint.

"It wasn't my plan," I say. "Lindsey?"

"Dead. They kept me as bait. Mostly this dude here," he says, nodding at the Hunter. "He took my memories, too."

Borrowed, the Hunter corrects. *I gave most of them back. But you've served your purpose. You've brought me the anomaly.*

"Anomal-what?" Michael says.

"He thinks I'm special," I explain.

"You're special, all right," Michael says. "Specially stupid to come back here."

"You mean 'especially,'" I point out.

"Shut up," Michael says.

I smile. It's good to have him back.

"Special," the Hunter says, ignoring us. "Much more powerful than he should be."

"He's the Chosen One!" Zack says. "He has the Spirit of the Warrior in him."

The Warrior? the Hunter mindspeaks. *What is this?*

"A god," Zack says. "Or half god, really. His spirit is in Jesse. . . ." His voice trails off, and his cheeks color.

The Hunter mindspeaks, *You are a very strange species.*

I say, "I'm not an anomaly. There are more like me. Some even stronger than me. You're in a lot of trouble here."

The Hunter seems even more amused. *I don't think so. If there were others more powerful than you, we wouldn't have been able to take over your planet in a matter of your* seconds. *There is nothing left for you to do but die. Do it with honor. Die well.*

The Hunter flicks his finger. Nothing more. Zack screams and falls. I manage to deflect the last of whatever the Hunter has shot at Zack, but Zack hits the ground hard.

Send me a message from the land of the dead, the Hunter mindspeaks.

Zack's dead? Before I can check, the Hunter flicks his finger at me and something happens. Instead of dying, I stumble into dreamwalking. I can't control it. I feel like I'm in a dream. The moment I'm in splits into a lot of different moments. I see, all at once, all these possible moments, each branching off from the one like streams from a river. And I see us die in all of them — every possible stream. Until I don't. Until, in just one, I don't see us die.

I've seen some strange things since the invasion, but this is by far the strangest.

Then I'm back in the main moment, no longer dreamwalking. It feels like I've been taken to some other place and brought back. Places. Some other places. I was more than myself, like I was somehow all the possible mes at once. And now I'm back.

And while I was gone, the Hunter's death ray completely missed me.

The Hunter looks perplexed, like he knows something just happened but he doesn't know what, and that hesitation gives me enough time to do the one thing that will lead to the moment in which we aren't killed. The one moment.

I join with Catlin. My dad, soldier and real warrior, used to say there was no weapon stronger than surprise. And the Hunter is definitely surprised.

Catlin and I create a whole room of the two of us — way more than the lousy dozen Hunters he produced earlier. Some of us run at the aliens and some of us run for the doors and some of us just stand there and make faces at the aliens. Stick out our tongues. Pull our mouths wide with our fingers. Laugh at them. It may be a little childish, but it's totally satisfying. Our power is awesome and it's different. I'm not sure how, but it is different from their power.

The Hunter, with the sweep of his arm, destroys all of the fake Jesses and Catlins. But we get lucky, just as I knew we would; the sweep of the Hunter's arm that kills the fake Jesses and Catlins also pops all the light-bulbs in the room, and the room goes dark. I'm ready for this, and somehow Catlin is, too, even though she hasn't seen how it all plays out. In the moment it takes for the hunters to turn their attention back to us, Catlin and I create more illusions, and this time we cloak ourselves—our real selves, and Michael and Zack, too. Using the fireman's carry, I lift Zack, and Catlin and I run for the door with Michael limping along behind us.

This is as far as I saw when I dreamwalked.

I don't see how we can make it to the car from here.

We do have one small advantage, though: their physical limitations, the whole Big Bird way of moving, will allow us to put a little space between us and them once they figure out that the real "us" have left the building. They're still able to kill from the other side of that space, but we'll make it a little harder on them.

When I think this through, it doesn't sound all that encouraging. "We'll make it a little harder for them to kill us" still has a definite bad-ending ring to it.

Then I notice all those ships in nice, neat lines. The aliens are certainly very neat. Neat and polite. You have to give them that.

"The ships," I say, steering Catlin toward them. Michael's limp is more pronounced now, but he just grimaces and hustles as fast as he can.

The Hunter attacks as soon as he steps out the door. I'm still joined with Catlin, though, and we deflect the attack. I can feel his surprise. We try a countermove that sends out a wave against him and the other hunters. It does actually knock a few hunters back. *The* Hunter easily blocks it, though.

Because we've stopped to fight, Michael's the first one to the ship, despite his limp.

"You never could run worth a damn," Michael says as I scramble onboard with Zack and Catlin.

"I was a little busy," I say, dumping Zack on the floor. "And I was carrying baggage."

It's crowded with four of us in the ship, but we make do. Catlin's mind is interfacing with the ship, and she uses its power to shield us just as the Hunter and a few other hunters attack again. Even with the shield, the ship rocks back and forth like a boat in a storm. Catlin gets us off the ground.

I work on a shield to add to the ship's shield, but I don't get much of one up before the Hunter's next attack hits us. My shield breaks and all the windows in the ship shatter and the ship spins out of control and into a tree. Miraculously, Catlin is able to get us out of the branches without tearing the ship apart.

"Can we join?" I shout at her over the sound of the wind whipping through the windows.

"I don't think I can do that *and* fly this thing!" she shouts back. "Just do whatever you can!"

I create another shield on my own while she flies us low across the road and toward a hill. It's not very strong. Not strong enough to block another hit from the Hunter.

But the hit never comes. We've moved out of the

Hunter's range. I hear him in my head, though. He says that a hunter loves the hunt and he'll be with me shortly.

Take your time, I mindspeak.

I glance down and see the hunters moving awkwardly toward their ships, but I know they won't be awkward once they're in them. I can hear them setting their controls. I can hear *him* loudest of all. He's excited.

"I can't fly this thing like they'll be able to fly their ships," Catlin says, hearing what I'm hearing. "I'm not that good yet."

"I know."

"What do you mean, you know?" she snaps. "You don't know."

"I just meant, you know, I know. I get it."

"It would help if you had more confidence in me," she says.

I've been drawn into these conversations before, so I should know better. I really should.

"But you said it first."

"I know what I said. I was hoping you would contradict me. Show a little faith."

"Uh," Michael says, "think maybe you guys could have this conversation later? Not when we have, you know, some aliens coming to kill us?"

"Coming fast!" Catlin shouts, looking back. "If Darth Vader gets close, he'll kill us this time. Our shield is pretty much destroyed."

"Darth Vader?" I ask. But now that she's said it, I can totally see it.

"Hey, Tex, this plan of yours for saving me . . ." Michael says. "I think the escape part needs a little work."

"And I think—" but I don't finish my thought because I feel the Hunter closing in on us. His ship is faster than the others—and definitely faster than our busted one.

"The river," I say. "Go to the river. Go toward where we parked our ship."

"Which way?" she says because she is seriously directionally challenged. She has one of those senses of direction that has no sense. I point, because she's also left- and right-challenged. She makes a sharp turn that throws us up against the left side of the ship. Her hand slips out of the control, and we drop. *Fall* might be more accurate.

Above us some kind of beam passes right where we were. The death rays.

"Good move," Michael says to Catlin.

Catlin gets her hand back in the control. She manages to get us leveled out just above some very solid-looking cedar trees.

The death rays change things. There's no way we have time to land the ship in the park.

"Get the ship higher, and aim north toward Dallas," I say, pointing north for her. "Set a course."

"I thought you wanted to head toward the park."

"Just do it."

I see what I think is the park as we come around the bend in the river. We've only got a few seconds before the other ships come around the bend, too.

"You guys can swim, right?" I ask.

"Of course we can swim," Catlin says testily. Michael doesn't answer. He just stares down at the river far below. I turn around and pull Zack, who is still unconscious, toward me.

"Why?" Catlin asks suspiciously.

"When I open the door, I want you both to jump," I say.

"Are you crazy?" Michael says. "I can't even see the river."

"That black inky stuff right below us? That's water."

"No way," Michael says.

"We don't have a choice!" I shout, wrestling Zack to the door. I fling it open. "Three, two, one . . . jump!"

Michael calls me several names. Rescued prisoners are definitely more grateful in movies. In a second we're all falling and there's no time for more names, no time for anything but fear and the intake of a breath.

I can feel the ship shoot up before we splash into the river. We hit the water hard but feetfirst, and the shock of the impact rouses Zack to semiconsciousness. We hit the bottom because the lake is so shallow, and I push off it back toward the surface. As we rise, Zack thrashes and pulls away from me. It occurs to me as we surface that we might have come up too soon. I half expect the alien ships to be hovering over us, the Hunter smiling in a satisfied way, but they aren't and he isn't. Catlin helps me with Zack, who is ineffectively splashing. Michael dog paddles alongside us, coughing and grunting.

The ships must have followed our ship because they're out of sight.

"I can't believe that worked," I say.

Michael finally gets a word out. It is not a nice one, but the effect is weakened as he coughs up another mouthful of water.

"Maybe you can run," I say to Michael, "but you aren't much of a swimmer."

"You noticed," he says.

As soon as we get to shore, Catlin works on Zack. I can't see what she does exactly. She moves in his mind. I can hear her, but his mind is a confused tangle to me. How she can find her way in there when she can't even tell north from south is a mystery.

"But you're from Florida," I say, standing over Michael. "You should be a good swimmer."

"Tallahassee, Tex. You ever heard of Tallahassee? What, you think all cities in Florida are on the coast?"

There's my poor geography putting me at risk for ridicule again.

"You could have said you couldn't swim instead of cursing me."

"They were going to kill us. Might as well drown as be blown up."

"Really?" I say. "I think being blown up would be way better. You'd go in an instant. Now, drowning, fighting for breath as water fills your lungs, that's worse to me. Way worse."

"Shut up," he says.

I smile. He's so easy to upset. I realize how much I've missed upsetting him.

"They say it's like going to sleep," I continue, "but who goes to sleep that way? Being slowly strangled by water."

"You should have just left me back there," he says. "The torture was nothing compared to this."

"I missed you, too," I say.

"Right."

"And I thought about it," I say. "I thought about leaving you there."

I can see his smile in the moonlight. "No, you didn't."

(((((21)))))

Catlin is still working on Zack, but I tell her we have to go. We pile into the ship, and Catlin flies up the river. We rise into the night sky, flying higher than the aliens like to. I'm sure the Hunter knows by now that the ship he's been following (or has destroyed) doesn't have anyone in it, but Dallas is north and we're traveling west; we've got a good head start. But just to add whatever help I can, I try cloaking us.

I don't have the ability Catlin and I have together, but I can still make it harder for them to find us. I make us a shadow in the night sky.

After everything that's happened, it's still the same night as it was when we left Taos. The sky above us still has all those stars dotting it, all those points of light. It seems kind of silly now to think we ever believed we were the only beings in the universe.

After ten or fifteen minutes, Catlin sets the ship course for Taos and then gets back to working on Zack. He still doesn't wake up, but at least he seems a little more stable, a little more comfortable, than he was.

Then Catlin turns her attention to Michael, who puts up a weak protest but quickly lets her do her healer thing. He's pretty beat up, and I know I can't even see the worst of it. I'm sure Michael didn't give his memories up easily.

I can see some of those memories as Catlin works on him. He remembers being killed, then waking and realizing he wasn't killed. He remembers Lindsey dying. He remembers me and Catlin and Lauren and some of our days as slaves. He doesn't remember escaping, though. And he can't remember whole sections of his life before he was a slave, either. All of that is gone.

He remembers the Hunter questioning him, getting inside him.

"He was too strong for me to keep out," Michael says. "But I couldn't tell him what he really wanted to know, which was where you'd gone."

His expression darkens, and he starts asking us where his mother's gone. His mother? I'm confused, and then I realize he's the one who's confused. He knows he should know this. He can't remember. He gets agitated, and he struggles to get up, rocking the ship.

Catlin does something that calms him. She sends

me a message asking me to put him to sleep. I touch his brow. He slumps in his chair.

"What just happened?" I ask.

"When they 'borrowed' his memories, they weren't careful about returning them. They did some damage."

"But you can fix him, right?"

"Maybe," she says. "I have to see how extensive the damage is."

"And Zack?"

"I don't know," she says again. "We'll see when we get back. Maybe with Running Bird's help . . ."

Her attention fractures, and at first I think it's because she's upset about Zack, but then I feel it, too—what's taken her attention—headed right toward us. We weren't being careful enough. And now it's too late.

I tell Catlin to go higher and see if we can get above the ship, but she says it's no use. They've already locked onto us.

I swear (sorry, Mom) and try to join with Catlin to create a shield. But a voice interrupts us. I expect it to say, *We're sorry for your loss.* Instead it says, *You're in big trouble, Chosen One. Land your frickin' ship.*

We land, and the other ship lands, and Sam rushes over. She tells us we're idiots. She lists our shortcomings: stupid, selfish, reckless, foolish—and did she mention selfish?

Catlin interrupts the lecture to say that we need to

get back to camp ASAP. "Zack is with us, and he's hurt, and we still have a long flight home."

But Sam says that Zack will have to wait. She says Catlin can work on him in the ship, but we're going to complete the mission. She didn't come all this way for nothing.

Catlin looks panicked. I'm not sure whether it's because of Zack or because she really, really doesn't want to head back to Lord Vertenomous's. *Again.*

"I can fly Zack and Michael back," she says. "You and Jesse can take your ship and go to Austin."

"No way," Sam says. "We need your ship, and we need you in case something happens."

"Why is it so important now?"

"You stirred them up, right? You had to fight to get your boy out."

"Yeah."

"They'll be on alert everywhere after tonight, but they won't expect us now. We need to build on what you did. We need to get their attention, let them know this invasion isn't over with yet, make them think twice. You two made a choice. Now I'm making one."

I think again about the man at the circus who may have been more than a man and his talk about choices. Could he have meant my choice to save Michael would cause Zack's death? But he said the beginning or end of choices. This isn't that. There's something up ahead (though Running Bird would say it's behind and beside at the same time) that will be a difficult and probably terrible choice. *Great,* I think, *another thing to worry about.*

Catlin isn't happy about going back, but it's pretty clear Sam is determined, so she walks back to the ship to try to make Zack as comfortable as possible. Michael steps out of the ship at the same time and stretches. I'm relieved to see him awake.

"What's the holdup?" he asks, eyeing Sam.

"This your friend?" Sam asks. "The one you risked all of New America for?"

"That's him," I say.

"Doesn't look like much."

"I grow on you," Michael says, an old, familiar grin splitting his face.

"Okay, Jesse's friend, come on, then. The least you can do is die for your new country. We're going to blow up some alien ships now."

"Awesome," Michael says.

"We'll see," she says.

"I always liked the Fourth of July," Michael says.

Am I seeing right? Is Sam actually smiling at Michael?

"It's not the Fourth of July," I say.

"Could be for all we know," Michael says, still smiling at Sam.

"Nope." I pull Betty's calendar out of my pocket. "It's not even the right month." I show them the marked-off days.

They both look at me like I've just spoken in tongues or something.

"You kept that?" Michael says. I can tell he remembers the day I got it. I wish for his sake that that was one of the memories the Hunter hadn't given back.

"That's strange," Sam says, looking at me through narrowed eyes.

"What?"

"One of the names for the Warrior is the Keeper of Days."

"It's just a homemade calendar," I say. "Besides, it was somebody else's before it was mine."

"Still," she says. "Strange coincidence."

"Whatever," I say.

"There are too many coincidences when you're around," she says. "Now, let's go blow some things up."

Sam has Michael fly with her. I fly with Catlin. We fly in a tight formation, side by side. Catlin tries to instruct me on how to help Zack sleep and fight the injury. I'm clumsy, but I do my best.

When we get close to Austin, Michael sends a message that Sam is worried about us being seen. He asks if Catlin and I can cloak. We cloak our ship and theirs.

I can hear Sam thinking, *This is unbelievable.* But

there it is again. The unbelievable is just one step from the believable.

My boy can't run worth a damn, but he's good at the alien stuff, Michael mindspeaks.

I run better than you can swim, I respond.

How do you do it? Sam mindspeaks.

They're like the ultimate power couple, Michael mindspeaks.

We aren't a couple, Catlin and I mindspeak together.

We land a few blocks away from the ships. Catlin and I stay joined and keep a cloak over us. The lot doesn't appear to be guarded. Everyone except Zack piles out of the ships.

We don't have any problem setting up the explosives. It becomes clear pretty fast that no one is guarding the ships. Who would attack them? The aliens are already back inside the palace, asleep.

We're safely back in our ships and hovering well above the parking lot when Sam detonates the explosives. They fire in a chain reaction, just like out of a movie. It's pretty awesome — lots of noise and fire and smoke. I keep expecting something bad to happen, the aliens to surround us or something, but this time everything is perfect. And it really is almost like the Fourth of July.

I fly back with Catlin, and we join and make a strong shield. It isn't long before we're out in the empty land of

West Texas. The enormous night is all around us. Then Michael starts to snore. I swear I can hear it all the way from inside the other ship. The old snorer guy back in New America will have an ally in his "Give me the right to snore or give me death!" campaign.

A few hours later, we reach the mountains. The sky is lightening, and the landscape is starting to take shape. By the time the sun shows itself, a bright orange orb rising in the east, we're passing over the adobe buildings of downtown Taos and the empty, narrow streets. We follow the windy highway up into the mountains toward the barn where we park the ships. Our whole trip has taken one night.

I look over at Catlin, exhausted from flying the ship and healing Michael and Zack and the battle at Lord Vertenomous's palace. She's done the most, pulled the most weight tonight. A lot more than me. Her hair has a definite lake-water fashion that I doubt will catch on but somehow makes her more beautiful. And what I think as I look at her is that I want to take away some of her burdens. To make things easier for her.

"He scares me," she says. "Darth Vader. He's as strong as Lord Vertenomous. We were lucky to get away from him. I'm afraid we won't be that lucky again."

"If we can get away from him once, we can do it again," I say. Sometimes you just have to say things you don't believe. I've learned that much.

"How'd you know how to do all that—make the decoys, I mean?"

"We did it together."

She shakes her head. "I followed what you did. I couldn't do it until I saw you do it."

I shrug. "It felt like both of us."

"You taught me. And something else happened, something before we joined, before you reached out for me."

"What?"

"I don't know," she says. "I felt you do something or change in some way."

I pretend I don't know what she's talking about, mostly because I don't understand it myself and I don't want to tell her about it and watch her expression get somber like she's adding this new talent to a list she's making. Did I really step ahead and back in time? Did I really see many possible futures? I couldn't. It's not something a human can do, even a talented human. But maybe a Warrior Spirit can. I can't pretend nothing is happening. Either I'm really going crazy (a definite possibility) or something beyond me took me to a place beyond me.

(((((22)))))

We take two cars up the mountain. I drive an old Oldsmobile, big as a tank. Michael rides shotgun, and Catlin falls asleep almost immediately in the back next to Zack. Sam's behind us in her truck. We follow the stream. It rushes down the mountain like it knows where it's going and is in a hurry to get there. Its energy makes me more tired. I can hardly keep my eyes open. Finally, we get to the ski lodge.

I park the car, and Sam pulls her truck up behind me. We all make the weary climb up the trail. I carry Zack part of the way, but Sam takes over after a while. She won't let Michael carry him, though he offers.

Michael asks questions about the rebels and the camp. He's surprised when he learns there have been those with talents all along and that Catlin is one of them.

"I did know there was something different about you, girl. I knew that much."

Zelda is in the big tent when we arrive. She comes running when she sees Sam carrying Zack.

"What have you done to him?" she shouts at me.

If looks could kill, hers would. There's no doubt about that. I'd be turned off in a second.

"He's going to be okay," Catlin says, though I know she doesn't know that. "He's unconscious right now, but he'll wake up soon."

"How could you take him?" Zelda says to me. "He's just a child!"

"He begged Jesse to let him come," Catlin says. "He wanted to fight."

"Zack is just a child," she says again. "You should know better."

"I'm sorry," I say. "He said he needed to. I thought . . . I'm sorry."

I should have put him to sleep down by the ships. I understood his wanting to go, and I let my understanding convince me to do something I knew I shouldn't. My father used to say you learn more from mistakes than from anything else. I've been learning a lot lately.

Zelda looks like she wants to keep yelling at me, which I probably deserve, but Catlin directs Sam to take Zack to the hospital tent. When I start to follow them, Zelda tells me to leave. Just leave.

"She's kind of cute," Michael says once the others are gone.

"Who, Zelda?"

"The angry one, yeah."

Typical.

"Maybe you should go in the hospital tent and get looked at," I tell him. "Maybe you'll get the chance to score some points."

"I would never do that," he says, but he heads for the tent.

As I'm about to go to my tent to sleep, I have the misfortune of seeing Doc. He motions me to come inside the tent where he sits. I consider pretending I don't see him, but I doubt that is going to work. Doc definitely does not look happy.

"I presume that is the friend you went to save?" Doc says, gesturing to where Michael disappeared into the hospital tent.

"Yeah. Michael."

Doc nods. "And Zack?"

"I don't know yet. Catlin's been working on him. I'm sorry."

"You'd better tell me what happened."

And so I do. I tell him about putting Lauren to sleep and bringing Catlin and Zack along. I tell him about rescuing Michael and our run-in with the Hunter. I tell him about the multiple moments and how I seemed to be able to follow the one in which we survived. And I tell him about Zack getting injured and Sam coming to find us. Finally, I tell him about the explosion back at the palace and how I think we managed to blow up most of the aliens ships parked there.

I try to explain why I had to go back for Michael. I don't know if I'm making much sense in my current state — I'm so tired I can hardly see straight — but when Doc tells me my punishment, he doesn't seem nearly as angry as I expected.

He assigns me a month on toilet-cleaning detail. Catlin, too.

"I talked her into going along," I say. "It wasn't her fault. It was all mine."

"Now she'll go along with you on toilet-cleaning duty. She should have had better sense. Lauren did."

Yes, she did, I think.

Doc lectures me about being a leader and about how I have to think about all of New America now. He reminds me, as Sam did, that my selfishness could have cost lives. His lecture isn't as impassioned as Sam's, but I feel even guiltier somehow. I don't like letting Doc down.

"You've got to grow up fast, Jesse," he says. "We won't make it if we don't start acting like a unit. Like a family."

I tell him I'll do my best. I mean it. But if I had to make the choice all over again about going to save Michael, would I change anything? No.

⟨⟨⟨⟨⟨ 23 ⟩⟩⟩⟩⟩

As I come out of the main tent, Michael comes out of the hospital tent. I ask him how Zack's doing.

"He still hasn't woken up. Catlin says he's fighting, but the longer he stays asleep, the less likely it is he'll wake."

"And Zelda?"

He looks uncomfortable. "Let's just say there's one less member in the Jesse fan club."

Then he tells me that the healer in there had a look at him and said she didn't think there was much she could do to help him recover his memories.

"I got the feeling Catlin disagrees, though. Our girl is a lot better doc than the healer they have here."

I'm not surprised to hear that. I take Michael to the check-in area to get him a tent and a sleeping bag.

"Michael!"

We turn and see Lauren, clutching her yellow pad and walking with a small group of people. Either New Bloods or SAFers, I imagine. But she quickly says goodbye to them and rushes over to us. She throws her arms around Michael and kisses his cheek.

"I can't believe it! We thought—I can't believe it. I'm so happy you're here!"

She doesn't hug me. She doesn't say she's happy I'm here. She says, "I guess you managed not to get yourself killed. Where are Catlin and Zack?" She looks around as if she expects them to follow me wherever I go from now on.

"Catlin's in the hospital tent," I say, "looking after Zack."

For a second, she looks concerned and sympathetic, but then she just looks pissed. "He's hurt?"

I nod.

"You shouldn't have taken him. You and Catlin going was bad enough, but taking Zack was stupid."

"I know," I say. "I screwed up."

"And I told Doc, in case you're wondering, that you'd taken a ship. He had to be told."

"I know," I say. "Look, I'm sorry about the . . . you know—"

"Knocking me out?"

"Yeah."

She says, "You should be sorry."

"I am." I am smart enough not to tell her that I'd do it again if I had to, but I think it. I shield the thought.

The conversation ends there. We have nothing more to say or too much more to say, and we stand there awkwardly, the silence just making everything more awkward. Finally I say I need to sleep and we need to get supplies for Michael.

"We'll meet up later," Michael says to Lauren. She tells him she's glad he's here, and then she turns and walks back toward the little group waiting for her.

"Was it my imagination, or was Lauren a little cool toward you?" Michael asks as we walk up the trail.

"You don't have an imagination," I say.

"That's what I thought. I guess she doesn't like you running off with Catlin."

"I didn't run off with Catlin."

"Dude. It looked like that was who you were with to me."

"Lauren was going to tell everyone we were leaving. She—"

"Was just being Lauren, Tex. I get it. Do you?"

"Did I really just save your butt?" I say. "What was I thinking?"

"You need a little reality check from the truth teller. You don't put girlfriends to sleep and then run off with other girls. It makes them mad."

"That's not the way it was." Though it's not factually incorrect. "Not reality," I insist.

"I think it's Lauren's reality."

He's probably right, which is totally irritating. But he doesn't get a chance to gloat because on the way up the path a bunch of people stop me to say they hope the Warrior Spirit is guiding me well.

Michael gives me a condescending look. "What's with all this Warrior Spirit stuff?" he says. "Zack acted like you were some kind of god."

"Well, half god," I say.

"Right," he says, and smiles but stops when he sees I'm not joking. "You're a half god now?"

"He's in me — sort of."

I tell him about the legend. "People are desperate," I say.

"They must be," he says.

I can't argue with that.

We get supplies for Michael and bring them back to our campsite. All I want is to get in my sleeping bag and sleep for a month. Michael, though, says he's going for a walk. He wants to breathe a little fresh air.

"Don't get lost," I say, unzipping my tent. "I don't want to have to come looking for you again."

"You get your sleep, Chosen One," he says. "You're gonna need it."

"The Warrior in me says good night," I say.

You'd think I'd be asleep in about two seconds, but I'm not. Lots of thoughts buzz around in my mind like irritating insects and keep me awake. Regret and worry about Zack. Confusing thoughts about Catlin and Lauren. Worry about Michael. Finally, though, exhaustion does win out, and I slip away.

I wake up like I've never been asleep at all, like I've just closed my eyes. And maybe I have. I hear minds outside my tent.

It's time for our training session, I hear someone mindspeak loudly.

I hear the minds all thinking about my trip to Austin, about how I went and got my friend and brought him back and how I defeated the aliens. Again. I hear hope.

Then I hear something farther off. A familiar voice. Soft. Lauren? I reach for it. I want to say I'm sorry. Tell her that I feel bad about everything and especially about what I did to her. About what I thought about her. About what I *didn't* think about her. Bad.

But I hear another voice close to hers. Dylan's voice.

"He would risk all of New America for one friend. He would see us all die. That's the person you think should lead us? That's the person you trust, Lauren?"

"I used to," she says. "When we were slaves and after we escaped, he was amazing. Now I don't know."

"New America needs a leader who thinks of everyone. I admit he's strong; he's a powerful weapon in fights with the aliens. But he can't be in charge. He will get us all killed. You know I'm right."

"I thought he might grow into it," she says. "I thought I could help him. But he doesn't want anyone's help. He's not ready. I can't pretend he's acted like a leader."

"I'm ready, Lauren," Dylan says. "I've trained all my life for this. We can agree to disagree about issues, but we agree about Jesse. You know we do. We have to protect New America. I can't do it without your help, without your advice. I'll need a group of advisors to help once I'm president, too. I'll need you."

Since when did Dylan become so patriotic about New America? He sounds so sincere I almost believe him. And Lauren—I can't really blame her for thinking I'm irresponsible. Still, I feel betrayed. How can she believe Dylan?

The minds outside my tent are getting impatient.

"Excuse me, sir. Are you awake in there?" someone says, someone young enough to think I should be called "sir."

I tell them to go to the training field, that I'll be right there. I get dressed and come out. My body aches, and I feel like I'm still half-asleep, my thoughts slow and uncertain, like I'm moving through a fog. I look around and see Lauren and Dylan down the trail. Lauren sees me and turns and walks away. Dylan looks back at me with a big smile on his face. I wonder if he's wanted me to hear them, if he somehow made it happen.

I go to the workout spot. I start off with some warm-up exercises. Everyone gets a good sweat going, and I encourage them to do these exercises on their own outside of class.

I tell them something I've been thinking about. "The aliens are slow. Physically slow. It may not seem like much of an advantage, but it is an advantage. It's a way we're better than they are."

We work through a lot of martial-arts drills. Hand drills. Elbow strikes. We do some different stances to work on control. We try a few kicks.

And this time, when I try to translate some of the physical moves into moves of the mind, some people start to see what I'm doing. Their movements are awkward and slow to me, but they do make solid attacks with the mind. It's a long way from what the aliens do, but it's a start.

Maybe Lauren and Dylan are right. Maybe I'd be better just training people to fight—be that "weapon" Dylan thinks I am. It's not like I want to be the leader of these people anyway. I just don't trust Dylan to be a good leader. I don't trust him, period.

(((((24)))))

The workout goes on for over two hours. Lauren shows up at some point, which makes me happy, and then Catlin and, at the very end, even Michael, though he just watches. I must have seventy or eighty people at the workout. Even some of Dylan's supporters show up.

Afterward, everyone else wanders away until it's just me, Lauren, Catlin, and Michael in the clearing. It should feel like a reunion, but instead it feels like we're walking through prickly cacti.

Lauren gives Catlin the same frigid look she gave me earlier.

"I guess you think because you got Michael out, everything is fine, right? I guess you both think that."

Catlin looks uncomfortable, but she doesn't look away. "I don't think that. But Jesse was right, and we got him back from them. You don't know what it's like to be in their power." She looks close to tears. "I should get back to the tent. Why don't you come with me, Michael? Let me examine you."

"Fine by me," Michael says with a grin. The tension eases just a bit.

"You'll let me know if anything changes with Zack?" I ask, even though I know she will.

"Of course," she says, then hurries Michael away down the path.

"Can we go for a walk?" I say to Lauren when it's just the two of us.

"I don't really have time. I'm supposed to type up some reports, and we're having the first meeting of New Bloods tonight. Are you even coming?"

"Of course," I say as if I'm hurt she'd think I wouldn't, though the truth is that I kind of forgot about the New Bloods meeting. But the air warms at least a whole degree. Okay, maybe a half. "I need to talk to you about what happened. Just a short walk?"

"Fine," she says, "but I've got to be back here in this spot in half an hour."

We walk over to the picnic area. "I'm really sorry," I say, sitting at one of the tables. She doesn't sit next to me. Instead she actually walks around the table and sits across from me. "I just did what I felt I had to do. You were going to stop me. I needed to get Michael. I made a decision, and I'm sorry it hurt you but I'm glad I did it."

Okay, the *but* definitely sends the temperature falling again. I try to add another *but* to get it to rise.

"But I am sorry, I really am, for what I did to you. It was wrong."

"I believe you," she says.

"Good."

"And if it was just me, I'd get over it."

"Who else is there?" I ask. I didn't knock out anyone else as far as I remember.

"Everyone. Everyone who is here in this camp."

"New America?"

"That's right. New America."

"I think they'll forgive me. They came to the workout. Some of them even congratulated me on getting my friend."

"You don't get it, do you?" she says, leaning forward.

"I guess I don't."

"You think about yourself first. I know you went back for Michael, but you did it because *you* wanted to. You wanted to save Michael, and you risked everything to do what you wanted. What if they'd captured you?"

"They didn't," I remind her.

"But what if they had and they'd gotten our position out of you?"

"I wouldn't have told them."

"Right. You forget I know how strong they are. People here think you're strong, but they don't know the aliens the way we do. The aliens are stronger. They would have forced you. Anyway, the point is you put your friend over the whole group. That's not a leader. A leader makes the difficult choices. If that means one has to be sacrificed to save the rest, then that's the way it has to be. You haven't learned to be a leader. And you may have caused one innocent boy's death."

She wields Zack's injury like a weapon, and maybe that's her right, but it makes me angry. "I never said I wanted to be a leader."

"No?" she says, raising an infuriating eyebrow. "Then tell me why you won't make people see that there is no such thing as the Warrior Spirit."

"I've told people," I say, but I don't sound very convincing, even to myself.

"You like it. You like them thinking you're destined to lead them and save them. You like that they think you're a strong fighter."

"I am a strong fighter," I say. I can't help it. She's so sure about everything, so self-righteous.

But there's something that bothers her more than the Warrior Spirit, more, even, than my crazy rescue mission to Austin. I can feel it in her, but she still surprises me when she says, "When I said we could lead together, you looked at me like I was crazy."

I frown. "No, I didn't. Or if I did, it's just because the idea surprised me. I hadn't really thought of myself as wanting to lead New America. I told you that."

"Right," she says. And then the thing that she's been holding in spills out: "You think that just because I don't have that much telepathic power, I can't lead. You're wrong, you know. I'm not like Catlin or you, but I know how to lead people and you don't. You or Catlin."

"And what about Dylan?" I say. "Does he know how to lead, too?"

For a second she looks a little guilty. Just a second. Just a little. Then she glares at me.

"I just know we can't trust you."

"You really believe that?"

She doesn't say anything. And in that silence is everything. I knew it before, I guess, but I didn't admit it. I do now.

"You're going to help Dylan?" I ask, because I need to hear her say it.

"He understands about leading."

"What about SAF?"

"I've been rethinking that, too. I was letting my feelings for you cloud my judgment. Stay and fight sounds like you. It's what you do well—fight. But what about everyone else? You saw us today during the training session. We can't fight them. Not fight and win. If we can't win, we have to change tactics."

"You don't know we can't win," I say, though I've thought the same thing many times.

"We both know," she says, standing.

"So you're going to help Dylan?"

"He's not as bad as you make him out to be. Anyway, he can lead these people. He wants to. You don't. You should be what you are, Jesse. Just stop pretending."

"Right," I say. I stop myself from saying "That goes two ways," and later I'm glad I didn't say it. It will seem like I did one little thing right.

"I've got to get going," she says.

"Okay."

"See you around, then," she says.

"See me around?"

"What do you want me to say?" she says sharply.

I don't have an answer.

She makes a little sound of contempt and strides off without looking back. I sit there in the middle of the forest and think how twisted everything has become. It was simple just a little while ago. I liked a girl. She liked me. Of course, there was the whole alien invasion, but I was, at least, sure about Lauren.

I feel tired. I feel so tired I can't imagine walking to my tent or even into the woods. I lean forward and rest my head in my arms on the table and drift off almost immediately.

25

We do see each other around. In fact, we see each other at dinner that night, but we don't sit together. She sits with Zelda. I sit with Catlin and Michael. She does come over to ask Michael to come to the meeting of New Bloods tonight.

"I hope you're still coming," she says to me.

I don't answer.

"What does she mean, 'still'?" Catlin says when Lauren walks off.

"We aren't together anymore," I say.

"Because of what we did?"

"Because of a lot of things."

"I'm sorry."

"Dude," Michael says, "I gotta say she didn't really seem exactly right for you. I wouldn't have said it before, but it's true." With typical Michael subtlety he adds, "Not your dream girl."

Catlin does her best to pretend that he hasn't spoken, and I do the same.

One of the healers who works in the hospital comes up and tells Catlin that Zack is awake. Catlin's face lights up. She says she'll let me know how he is as soon as she can, but if he's awake that's huge.

Catlin starts toward the hospital.

"Are you coming?" Catlin asks the healer.

The girl shakes her head. "Go on ahead. I'm going to grab a cup of coffee."

"Okay. I'll see you there," Catlin says.

But the girl doesn't head toward the coffee. Instead she lingers at our table. I look over at Michael, wondering if he's been talking the girl up.

"Want to sit with us?" I say.

She shakes her head.

"I heard you and Lauren broke up," the girl says.

"News travels fast in a telepathic rebel camp," Michael says.

The girl's looking at me. "Is it true?" she asks.

"I don't really want to talk about it."

She frowns. "Do you even know how amazing Catlin is? We have a healer at the hospital. A good one. And her daughter, too, who was training to be one before the invasion. Catlin can do things our healer could never consider doing. She's totally brilliant. No one else could have brought Zack back."

"I know she's good," I say, a little confused about why she's telling me this.

"Not just good. My mother is good. I'm good. Catlin is amazing. You'd better not hurt her."

The girl walks away and leaves me sputtering. "What was that all about?"

Michael shakes his head. "I guess you know what you're doing."

I put down my fork. I'm not hungry anymore. "Not really."

"I was just being nice," he says. "You've never known what you're doing."

"Thanks."

"Welcome. Looks like everyone but you can see the obvious."

"Can we just talk about something else?" I say.

He says we can as long as it doesn't have anything to do with little green aliens.

We argue about which superhero would win the decathlon if there was a Superhero Olympics. It feels like one of our old arguments. He says Superman, which I call an obvious and uninspired choice.

"Of course it's obvious, because anyone with half a brain would go with Superman."

"I guess you're proof of that."

"Who do you think then, Chosen One?"

"Thor, god of thunder."

"He's not a superhero."

"Son of Odin."

"Not a superhero. A god, I think. A *full* one."

"Some people would call him a superhero."

"Shut up."

26

Michael and I go up to the hospital tent to see Zack. Zelda is already there. Zack is sitting up on his cot.

"I was just telling Zelda how totally awesome you and Catlin were," Zack says. "You saved me. Then she saved me."

Catlin smiles at him.

"He didn't save you," Zelda says to Zack. "He put you there in the first place."

Zack shakes his head. "I wanted to go. I begged him. And when that alien struck me, Jesse did something. He turned his strike somehow. If it had hit me full-on, I'd be dead."

Zelda doesn't seem impressed.

"Catlin says I can leave tomorrow," Zack says. "I'm going to start training with you again as soon as I can. I'll be ready for the next fight."

"Good," I say. "That's good."

I say we'd better get going and let him rest. Catlin says she has one more patient to see. She'll see us back at the camp. I don't even notice Zelda is following us out until we're outside the tent.

"I'm not going to thank you for preventing his death when you're the reason he was there in the first place."

"I don't expect—"

She holds up her hand.

"Just listen to me. He worships you. He thinks you're some kind of hero. Just don't you ever put him in a place where he can be killed again. Don't you ever do that."

I want to say okay. I want to tell her that from now on, Zack will be safe. That she'll never have to sit by his cot again and worry that he might die. But in spite of what Lauren thinks, I do know that there will be hard choices ahead.

"You know I can't promise you that," I say as gently as I can.

Her face gets even more angry. She walks back into the tent.

Michael and I start down the path toward our campsite. Sam and Dylan come walking up it. Better than Lauren and Dylan, I guess, but still not great.

Sam says, "You guys headed to the town meeting?"

"I guess," I say.

Dylan's eyes lock onto mine. "I need a word with the Chosen One first," Dylan says. "You go on ahead."

"Come on, Jesse's friend," Sam says.

"My first town meeting ever," Michael says as they walk off. "Maybe you could guide me through it."

"What do you want?" I say to Dylan.

"I want you to go away."

"I want you to do a few things I doubt you'll ever do, too."

He pauses, as though he's deciding whether it's worth trying to explain himself to me. Lucky me. He seems to decide it is. "Even when I was a kid, I knew I'd do something great. I saw how my people were so careful because they were afraid. I had big plans for my clan and house. We wouldn't have just wasted our talents like my dad's generation and those before it, and we wouldn't have hidden them, either. We would have used them. We would have made people understand we weren't the freaks, the misfits; we were what humans could become. We were the future."

"The future how?"

"I would have joined the houses. Together we would have been too strong for the untalented. We would have improved mankind, taken it to a new level."

"Like the master race?"

He doesn't answer. "We're still the future, and I'm

still the leader. I'm the one chosen to unite us. I've known it since I was a child."

"You'd be like a king," I say.

"You can help," he says. "I would be grateful when I'm the head of the houses."

"Who doesn't want a king to be grateful to them?" I say.

"Think about it," he says. "Think about your friends. These are dangerous times. I will be the head of the houses. It's going to happen. You can be my friend or my enemy. The choice is yours."

"What was that all about?" Michael asks when I come into the meeting-hall tent.

"He wants to be my blood brother," I say, "or he wants my blood. I'm not sure which, but I'd bet on the second."

Sam says, "He's dangerous. I'd be very careful."

"Did you know he had this big plan," I say, "for uniting the houses and becoming king? He thinks it's his destiny or something."

"I'm impressed," she says. "I didn't know he had that much imagination."

"Oh, he's been imagining all kinds of things," I say.

"It's not much of a kingdom anymore," she says.

"It's a disappointment, but he'll take what he can get."

"On another topic, I have an idea for a second suicide mission," Sam says, clearly done talking about Dylan. "Your friend here has already volunteered."

"I did?" Michael says.

"You're probably still having memory problems," she says. "You were all for it."

"That doesn't sound like me," he says.

"We all surprise ourselves sometimes."

"What is it?" I ask.

She wants to attack Denver, where the aliens have a base. This time we'll do it right, she says. We'll take two trucks with soldiers, some of them pilots. We'll do more damage, get more ships.

"But first we need more explosives," she says. "Lucky for you, it just so happens I know where to get them — the safe house for the Wind Clan just outside the square in Santa Fe. We'll take the two ships, but just four or five people total. A quick in-and-out without anyone seeing us. We'll go tomorrow night, and then the next night we'll blow up the base in Denver."

I see Catlin making her way over to us. I see Lauren whisper something to Zelda from across the way, but I keep my shield up so that I don't have to hear whatever it is she says.

Sam lets Catlin know she's volunteered for a suicide mission. "Congratulations, you've been accepted."

"Lucky me," Catlin says.

The town meeting is shorter than the one last night. Everyone seems weary at first—camp life and the strain of being hunted, I think. I do hear a lot of buzzing about Michael, which becomes almost deafening when Doc calls him up to the stage to be introduced and welcomed into New America. Then there's news about our successful attack in Austin and some cheering over that. It's a small victory, but every victory makes us feel a little stronger. There's a moment of silence for all we've lost.

When the meeting is over, Michael, Catlin, Sam, and I walk back toward our campsite, but Sam turns off before long. Her tent is in the neighborhood closest to the food.

"It's where the best people live," she says, "but your hill is nice, too, if you don't mind walking."

As she walks away, Michael stares after her. "I'm in love."

"I thought you were in lust—I mean in love—with Zelda," I say.

"Who's Zelda?" Michael jokes, still staring at the spot where Sam was.

When we reach our campsite, I notice that Lauren's

tent is gone, which isn't exactly a surprise but still bothers me. Catlin looks at the empty space and then says she's going to turn in. She's exhausted. We say good night. It feels a little awkward between Catlin and me now, which bothers me, too.

"You think she likes me?" Michael says.

I'm thinking about Lauren and Catlin.

"Who?"

"Who do you think? The Amazon woman."

"Sam? Not particularly, but maybe you'll grow on her."

"I think she sort of likes me," he says, unzipping his tent.

I wish I had his confidence sometimes. I'm really tired. I don't realize how tired until I get inside my tent. I don't even take off my clothes or unzip my bag. I just lie on top of it fully dressed, and in a second I'm asleep.

At breakfast the next morning, I see that Lauren has joined Dylan and his sidekicks at the Dylan-and-his-sidekicks table. They seem very cozy, sitting there beside each other, talking—making plans, I suppose. Lauren is always making plans.

"Why is Lauren sitting over there with that creep Dylan?" Zack asks. He was released from the hospital tent first thing this morning, and we haven't had the chance yet to catch him up on what he's missed.

Zelda, who is sitting next to him but looking none too happy about it, tells him to be quiet and eat his breakfast. He's taken two helpings of everything, which seems like a good sign to me.

"What's that saying about a woman scorned?" Michael says.

"I didn't scorn her," I say. "If any scorning was done, she did it."

Zack gets it and doesn't seem all that upset. "She wasn't right for you anyway," he says with his mouth full.

Zelda scolds, "Stay out of it, Zack."

"It's true," he says defensively.

"It doesn't matter," Zelda says. "You don't necessarily say something just because it's true." Then she looks at me. "Sorry."

"It's all right," I say, and then I look at Zack. "It's all right, Zack. I'd rather hear the truth."

"Sure you would," Michael says.

Catlin gets up. "I've got to get to the hospital."

I hear Lauren laugh. Lauren's laugh is one of those musical ones. She could give a concert with that laugh. Right now she's giving a concert for Dylan.

"I've never heard Dylan be funny," I say to Michael. "Does he look like someone who could be funny?"

"Not intentionally," Michael says.

One thing about Michael: he's a good judge of character. Another thing: he's loyal.

That afternoon I train the faithful again. There are even more rebels at this session. Over a hundred, I'd guess. Zack's been telling everyone how I defeated (this is so the wrong word, but that's the word he uses) the great alien hunter and how I saved him. He claims he felt something in me that was like a sudden explosion of power.

"Like the spirit," he says.

Once again, I try to link the physical moves (roundhouse kick, tiger mouth, knife-hand strike, palm-heel strike, elbow strike, punches) with the moves of the mind. People do make the connections, but they make them imperfectly. I try not to be too disheartened. In tae kwon do it was the same. You have to do thousands and thousands of side kicks before you start doing them well. We do get a good workout, at least. This is my kind of sweating, good physical exercise, not sitting around nearly naked in a sweat lodge with a fat old dreamwalker.

After the punches and kicks, we work on hapkido moves. I've partnered everyone up so they can practice different techniques. We're working on a simple way to twist a wrist so the opponent is disabled.

One of the pairs is a guy named Lucas and a girl named Marie. I've seen Lucas hanging around with Dylan's group, though I'm not sure if he's really a part of it. I keep an eye on him because he's aggressive. I'm watching him when he twists Marie's wrist too much during the exercise. Marie stifles her cry of pain, but I can hear it in my mind.

I send someone to go get Catlin, and then I ask Lucas

what happened. He says it wasn't his fault; she moved when he had her in the hold and twisted her own wrist. Marie rolls her eyes.

"What's the big deal?" Lucas says. "It's not like it's broken."

Things like this do sometimes happen in a martial-arts class. They shouldn't, but they do. It's the way Lucas acts like it's nothing that irritates me.

I say I'll be Lucas's partner for the next technique, which is throwing. We've practiced how to fall, but I still make everyone go slowly. I help people get the throw right first and then come back to Lucas, who decides he's going to show people he's powerful, too, and throw me hard. I hear him think this. He has his shield up, but I hear right through it.

He steps into me and turns his body as I've shown him to do and grabs my arm, and then I do something that I hadn't planned: I use my mind to counter the move. He falls, exactly as he would fall if I had done the counter physically. But I didn't do it physically. I did it with my mind.

Lucas looks up at me. I think he's going to be angry, but he says, "Awesome, dude. How'd you do that?"

I try to teach them, but while some of them can use the move to stop another person, to put them down, none of them can actually flip someone.

Still, the group's progress is undeniable. In just a few days, they've gone from barely being able to do round-house kicks to being able to affect others with just their minds. I feel good about this.

After the training session, Catlin and I do our latrine duty. We've been shown how to use bleach and lime and the other cleaning materials. It's terrible work, but it makes me feel better to do it, like I'm paying something—not enough, but something—for stealing the ship and putting Zack in danger.

When we're done, Catlin and I wash up in the stream down from camp and then walk up the trail a ways and stretch out on some flat rocks in the late afternoon sun. I close my eyes and enjoy the feeling of the sun on my face.

"So," she says, "you and Lauren are over?"

"Seems like we barely got started," I say. "She said I was too selfish. And I can't be trusted. I don't know, maybe she's right. Maybe I am selfish. I could have gotten Zack killed."

"You didn't, though. Zack's fine. And Michael's here."

"We were lucky."

"It's more than luck," she says. "You need to quit saying that. You saved Michael, and you saved me, too. I thought I'd never get out of Lord Vertenomous's. I didn't think it was possible. So maybe Lauren doesn't know what she's talking about."

I turn my head to look at Catlin. But before I can say anything, it happens again: we join. We don't mean to; it just happens. Maybe because we're lying on this big flat rock, side by side, so close we're almost touching. And it's not like joining for fighting or hiding either. It's different.

"Am I interrupting?" a voice asks.

We both jump back. Mentally, I mean. Physically, we just sit up. To anyone who sees us, it doesn't look like we were doing anything. But it's not just anyone who sees us. It's Running Bird. And he sees more than just the physical.

"What?" we both say at once.

"Of course not," we both say at once.

We aren't joined anymore, but it sure sounds like we are. Catlin blushes and says she'd better go get cleaned up for dinner.

"You don't have to leave," I say to her.

"I definitely need to wash off our punishment more thoroughly before I go anywhere near food," she says. "I'll see you down there."

Running Bird says, "You both do still smell a little."

"Thanks," Catlin says.

She walks off down the path.

"So, what can I do for you?" I ask.

"I think the question is, what can I do for you, Warrior Boy?"

I frown. "I'm good, thanks."

"Are you sure about that?"

Then I realize I do want to talk to him. How did he know before I knew?

"Fine," I say. And I tell him about what I saw at Lord Vertenomous's place, about how I saw a lot of different possible futures and was able to choose the best one.

"You saw alternatives?"

"I guess."

"Can't be," he says. "The book is the book. What's written is written."

I shrug. "Maybe it's open to revision."

"The book is the book," he says.

"I saw different versions," I said.

"You making this up? You mad because I caught you and that pretty girl making out?"

"What?" I sputter. "I wasn't. I wasn't doing anything with her. And I'm not making this up."

"You finally ready to admit you got the Warrior Spirit in you?" he says.

"It could just be another talent," I argue. "Like dreamwalking."

"Never heard of any talent like the one you're

talking about. I have heard of a talent that a great holy man had once, though. He was able to move things with his mind. If you can walk through time, maybe you can move things with your mind."

"I was able to throw someone with my mind," I admit reluctantly.

"You stand right there," he says.

He walks about ten paces away, picking up rocks along the way. He turns around and throws a pebble at me. It hits me right in the forehead.

"Hey!"

He throws another pebble, a little larger this time, and I block it with my hand.

"Thing that holds large body of water *you*!" I shout.

"Thing that holds water? Pathetic cursing. You must have really loved your mother."

"Just stop throwing rocks. This is stupid."

"Bigger one coming."

I bat it away, but it cuts my hand. "Ow."

"Stop resisting, Warrior Boy," Running Bird says.

"I'm warning you," I say.

"Big one coming."

He throws a rock about the size of a baseball. I see it come at me, fast. Too fast to knock it away with my hand. And so I do what he's wanted me to do all along: I block it with my mind. Then I slice it into four pieces and send them flying back at Running Bird. He curses as they hit him with deadly accuracy. Well, not deadly, but hard enough to cause him a little pain and, I hope, discourage further rock throwing.

"You can't keep denying it, Jesse," Running Bird says. I don't think he's ever used my real name before. That scares me almost as much as what he says next: "You *are* the Chosen One."

(((((29)))))

At dinner I don't say anything to my friends about my little talk with Running Bird. Because even though I still don't totally believe in the Warrior Spirit, I can't deny it feels like something beyond me is helping me, some higher power.

Sam joins us at dinner. She brings along three other girls who she says can do a decent job of flying the alien ships. "They'll be coming with us to Denver tomorrow," she says. "I thought you all should meet one another."

I've been so distracted by my talk with Running Bird that I've totally forgotten about tonight's mission. "Doc is okay with this plan?" I ask doubtfully.

"I haven't been able to talk to him," Sam admits. "The healer won't let anyone in his tent."

"Marta won't even let me in," Catlin says. "She says she's been taking care of Doc for years and she doesn't need any girl's help."

"But you're better than she is," I say.

Catlin shrugs. "She's possessive about Doc. She's not that way about any of her other patients. Maybe I'll try again when we get back."

"We'll just have to go ahead as if Doc approves," Sam says. "I'll talk to him before the mission to Denver."

The sun is nearly down, and Sam says it's time to get going.

The three girls are a little angry they don't get to go on this mission, but Sam manages their egos by saying, "You three are too important for this. Tonight is nothing. Tomorrow is the big day. Get yourselves ready for tomorrow."

They aren't happy about it, but her explanation sends them off to their table. We start off down the trail to the ski lodge.

"You guys, wait!" Zack calls, panting as he runs down the trail.

"No way, Zack," I tell him before he launches into his plea. "Not this time. You're still recovering from the last mission. Besides, your sister would kill me."

"It's not that," he says. "Running Bird sent me to come get you. All of you. Dylan's called a special meeting because Doc is sick."

Sam frowns. "What's this meeting all about?"

"Dylan wants to take control of New America. No election. He says his father's too sick. Running Bird says you guys need to be at the meeting."

Sam swears. We follow Zack back up the mountain and get to the meeting as Dylan and Running Bird take the stage. Dylan sees us, and I can feel his surprise and frustration.

Dylan wants to talk right away, but Running Bird says that the meeting must begin with a prayer, that all meetings need to begin with thanks to the gods for another day.

I can feel the frustration in Dylan intensify.

After the prayer, Dylan gets right to the point. "My father has been sick for a long time. Most of you know he's had one heart attack. He suffered another yesterday. The healer is with him now, and she will update us when she knows more. But even if he survives, the responsibility of being the leader of New America is too much for him. You all know my father. He won't say he can't do it. He'd rather kill himself trying. Look, it's time he took care of himself for once. I am ready to take over for the good of New America. I'm ready to do what I was raised to do. Let me."

Then one of his sidekicks stands up. No, not one of his sidekicks. Lauren. Lauren stands up. "I nominate

Dylan for provisional president until we can get to the caves and hold a legal election."

There's a lot of mental mumbling. Dylan raises his hand for silence. "Lauren has helped me see that we are one house now, the House of New America. We are the future. Let me lead us to a place where we can survive. Let me lead you into the future."

Lauren speaks again. "I've heard some people say that the next leader of New America should be Jesse because he has these powers that we've never seen before. He can kill just like the aliens can! But there is more to being a leader than being a good fighter. Jesse is my friend, and he is many good things, but Jesse is not a leader. He's wrong about staying and fighting. I see that now. There are too many of them. Jesse will get you killed. It's that simple."

Wow, I think. She's good. She's a powerful ally. I should have told her I knew she would be. I should have told her that I would have been proud to lead with her if I'd wanted to lead. I should have told her a lot of things.

Dylan tells the crowd that he will lead them to safety. He orders them to pack up.

Running Bird holds up his massive arms. The crowd noise dies away. "Not so fast," he says. "New America is a democracy. Leadership positions are not automatically inherited. Even in the House of Jupiter, you could not just appoint yourself. We must wait for Doc to get better."

"What if he doesn't?" Lauren says.

"Either way," Dylan says, "I'll only be acting president. There will be an election eventually. But now we need to move out."

"I say we vote!" Sam shouts.

I hear a lot of people agree immediately. Some disagree. Then others chime in, agreeing. Like old America, there's a lot of difference of opinion.

Dylan takes his seat with a pinched look of annoyance on his face, and Lauren takes her seat next to him. They both shoot daggers at Sam—well, figurative ones.

Dylan wants to be king. He plans on it. Lauren probably does believe there will be elections later, but there won't be. Once Dylan becomes the head of New America, he'll stay the head. He'll rule this little kingdom and wait for a chance to expand it. He'll be a terrible king, like one of those tyrants. Unfair. Selfish. Eventually paranoid and murderous. I see Dylan clearly.

"I nominate Running Bird!" I shout.

And the old son-without-a-mother actually looks surprised. For once he doesn't know what to say. I enjoy that. A lot.

"I second the nomination," Catlin says quickly.

"Third," Sam says.

Dylan is indignant. I can tell that he expected someone to nominate me, and that after Lauren's rousing speech, it'd be no contest. But Running Bird has more supporters among the crowd than Dylan is prepared for.

Dylan stands up, and the confused chatter of the crowd quiets. "I can see that people are confused," he says. "Perhaps now is not the time to be voting. We should wait until we have the report from Marta. Hold the election in a few days, after people think it over."

This sounds reasonable, which makes me suspicious.

"Doc is still our leader," Running Bird says. "Let there be no more talk of voting for a new leader until that is no longer true."

The meeting breaks up. The sudden shift by Dylan worries me.

"What's he up to?" Catlin says.

"Nothing good," Sam says.

I'm pretty sure she's right, but what about Lauren? I'm angry with her, but I know she wouldn't do anything to hurt New Americans. He's fooled her. He must be very good to fool her. This worries me even more.

30

Sam, Michael, Catlin, and I head back down the mountain to the red barn. Everyone seems eager to talk about anything other than what just happened at the meeting. So Michael and Sam start discussing how some people are so poor at breaking up that they drive old girlfriends into the arms of first-class jerks.

"I didn't break up with her," I point out.

"Dude, you knocked her out and left with another girl," Michael says—and not for the first or even the tenth time. More in the twenty range.

I'm glad it's dark and I can't see Catlin's face and she can't see mine.

"I'd call that a bad breaker-upper," Sam says.

I turn to Michael. "I suppose you're a good breaker-upper."

"I'm excellent. My friends used to all come to me for advice. It's all in the tone of voice. Of course, I never knocked anyone out. I'm not sure even I could smooth that over."

"I didn't knock her out to break up with her! I did it because I was trying to save *you*. We all make mistakes."

"Even though you're probably the worst breaker-upper ever," Sam says as though I never said a word, "I think her joining Team Dylan is going too far."

"She didn't join Team Dylan because I broke up with her. And I didn't even break up with her." The conversation is too reminiscent of ones I've had with Running Bird. "Anyway, Lauren's right about me. I'm not leader material. But Dylan, he's, he's—"

"A sociopath," Sam says.

"A sociopath?" I say doubtfully.

"Charming boy," she says. "Nice smile. Smart. Just don't let your sister or your daughter or your dog near him."

"Dog?" Michael says.

"A girl got the better of him once. Made him look foolish. Next week her dog died. Poisoned. Poor thing had been fed fishhooks in hamburger. That dog loved hamburger."

I can see the dog writhing on the floor, see Sam see him, and see her drop to her knees and hold the dog and cry as she snaps his neck.

"She could never prove Dylan had done it, of course, but she knew what he'd done. Old Yeller was his name. Stupid name. I loved that dog."

She stares straight ahead. I know that look. Holding yourself still because you're afraid any movement will be too much.

"He almost did it," I say. "He almost just took over."

"Running Bird is powerful, but everyone knows he's cracked up before," Sam says. "They won't trust him. Even I'd worry he couldn't take the pressures of leading us. This isn't just Sunday picnics and house politics. It's war."

We're all quiet. We know she's right.

"I need to tell Lauren about Dylan," I say. "She needs to know."

"Maybe I should tell her," Michael says. He's probably right. She's more likely to listen to him than me.

"Tell her," Sam says, "but don't expect her to believe you. Dylan is good at getting people, especially girls, to do what he wants. He's hard to expose. Believe me, I've tried."

31

We fly to Santa Fe, Catlin and me in one ship and Michael and Sam in another.

It's on the way there that I have a premonition, a bad feeling. I do a scan and ask Catlin to do one, but neither of us feels anything. Nothing.

But then I feel the bad feeling, danger, again, and this time I feel him: the Hunter.

"He's here," I say to Catlin, and we join almost without thinking. "Get us on the ground. Those trees down there."

She does, and Sam follows. We land and get out of the ships. Sam's drawn her automatic.

"What is it?" she says.

"The Hunter," I say. "He's here." *Only he isn't.* We're looking all around, but there are no ships. There are no aliens.

"Are you sure?" Sam says.

"Of course I am," I say.

"I don't feel anything," Michael says.

"Me, neither," Catlin admits.

I can't believe I'm wrong. I know I felt him. I know it. I think about him, try to concentrate, to feel him out. Instead I hear my father's voice. It says something that seems to have nothing to do with the Hunter. It says, "A good soldier always has a contingency plan." At first I kind of brush this off, but then I think about it again. The Hunter is a good soldier. So what would the Hunter's contingency plan be?

I turn to Catlin. "Could the Hunter have planted something on Michael?"

"Like what?"

"I don't know exactly. Some kind of tracking device maybe."

"Sure. It's possible."

"Wait, what?" Michael sounds outraged.

I ignore him and stay focused on Catlin. "Wouldn't you have seen it, though, when you were treating him?"

"Not necessarily. I wasn't looking for it. And to be honest, I'm not sure I would know it even if I found it. Sanginian talent is so advanced."

"No way," Michael says. "I'd know. I'd feel something. Wouldn't I?"

"But that would mean . . ." Sam says.

"Jesus," Catlin says.

Michael looks stricken. I can hear him thinking again that he would know — but what if he didn't?

"It was his contingency plan," I say. "The Hunter's. In case we somehow managed to get Michael out of there. That way even if he lost, he could still win. He could track Michael."

"Not just Michael," Catlin says. "All of us."

"All of us, then. It doesn't matter. We've got to go back."

We pile into our ships and set a course for the camp. Catlin and I join again and put up a shield.

"We have to get Running Bird a message," I say.

"How?"

"I don't know. If I could fall asleep or if we were in a sweat lodge, maybe I could dreamwalk."

"I don't think we have time for you to fall asleep."

I try to think of Running Bird. What would he do? He'd probably tell me to stop whining and start acting like the Chosen One. Find the Warrior Spirit in me. Use it.

"Push me," I say to Catlin.

"Push you?"

"Give me a push out of the ship."

"I don't think that's a good idea."

"Mentally. Push me mentally. Send my essence, or whatever it is, falling."

"Still a bad idea," she says.

"Stay joined with me. It will be like bungee jumping. You'll be the cord that yanks me back."

"It's too dangerous," she says.

"We don't have a choice," I say. "I need you to trust me. Push. Now!"

So she pushes. I call the Warrior Spirit, which feels kind of like shouting off a cliff and waiting to hear something besides an echo. I don't hear anything but my voice, but I do fall. I fall very fast. I still don't feel any Warrior Spirit.

"I'm pulling you back!" Catlin shouts.

"Don't!" I shout.

I send her a picture of the camp destroyed. It's not real. I make it up. It looks pretty real, though. And she gets the message. She lets me go.

I'm more in control now, more flying instead of falling. I picture Running Bird, because somehow I know that this is how I get to him. I imagine his large arms and that muffin-top stomach, the brown spots on his hands and face, the long white ponytail.

I see him in his tent, which is up above the camp, near his sweat lodge. He's sitting in his tent, and he's holding something in his hands and staring at it. It's a picture, I realize. Him and Doc and a woman. They're all young.

"Running Bird," I say.

He looks up. At first he doesn't see anything, but

then he looks in a different way. I can feel him do it. He sees me.

"You asleep?" he asks.

"No. Listen—"

"Didn't think so. You're dreamwalking, but you aren't dreaming. You're getting to be a regular prodigy, Warrior Boy."

"The Hunter," I say.

"What?"

I'm being pulled away, pulled back up. Catlin is pulling me back. I try to tell her to stop, but she's too far away. "The Hunter!" I shout at Running Bird just before I'm yanked up out of the tent.

I'm back in the ship.

"Why'd you pull me back?" I shout at her.

"You were slipping from me. I almost lost you."

I was so close. "I don't know if he understood."

"But you made it. How is that possible?"

"I don't think it was me," I admit. "I mean, I think I had some help."

She nods. She thinks so, too, I guess.

"I'm going to pray that he understood," she says.

We don't talk much after that. We speed through the blue moonlight. She prays to her gods. I don't know for sure that there's a Warrior Spirit in me, but I'm pretty sure what I just did was a leap of faith. So I thank him for his help and pray he will help us again.

(((((((32)))))))

The camp is gone. I can feel it before we land, and the feeling only gets stronger as we drive up the mountain in Sam's truck. Catlin and I make one of our best shields, and it's a good thing because we see ships in the sky over us. One, then two, then another pass right above us. The third slows but keeps going. We get to the ski lodge, hide the truck, and hurry up the trail.

We approach from the side with the densest woods and work our way above the camp so we can get a good view of it. Even though I expected it to be bad, the sight of scattered objects, mostly missing tents, and smashed machinery from the main tent still disturbs me. This was our home, and it isn't anymore. But then I realize I don't see scattered bodies—which I would if the New Americans had been caught by the hunters—and I feel better. They escaped. That's something. Everything, really.

A few aliens mill about, but they don't detect us. We're well hidden by the woods and our shield.

"Where is everybody?" Michael asks, whispering even though he could shout and the aliens wouldn't hear him.

"They got away," Catlin says. "Jesse warned them."

"How?" Sam asks, looking at me intently.

"I dreamwalked," I say. "I managed to find Running Bird. I guess he understood my warning."

"Maybe you really are the Chosen One," Sam says, but her usual sarcasm is unnervingly absent.

"Where would they go?" Catlin asks Sam.

"Doc had another camp on the south side of Taos," Sam says. "It's not as nice, but that's where we were supposed to meet if anything happened."

Before we go, Catlin slips into Michael's mind to try to find the tracking device. It takes her twenty minutes to find it. It's not a device at all, though. More like what Catlin would call a spell. The Hunter is connected to Michael. Catlin breaks the connection.

We hike back down to Sam's truck, and Catlin and I weave a cloak over it, then we drive down the main road and into Taos, none of us saying a word. There are aliens patrolling around camp, but once we get by them, the road is clear. We're lucky the hunters aren't around. We're lucky.

(((((33)))))

The new camp is rough and unmade and nothing like the old camp. Everyone looks like they've had a bad night. Some people are sleeping, curled up on the ground. Others just sit in small groups, looking dazed.

They do look glad to see us, though. An old man says, "Running Bird said the Warrior Spirit in you flew to him and warned him. We escaped just in time. Thank you, Warrior Spirit."

Others thank me. Or they thank the Spirit of the Warrior in me, anyway. People seem lifted a little by this hope that the Spirit is stirring in me and helping them, but I feel a familiar feeling, too: loss. It's all over this camp. We'd started to think of our former camp as home, but there is no home.

"Where's Running Bird?" I ask the old man who spoke to me.

"He is with Dylan, preparing for the funeral."

Catlin groans softly.

"Doc?" I say.

Then I realize that it's not just the loss of the old camp that I've been sensing but of Doc as well. He led a lot of these people into the mountains after the invasion and kept them alive, and now he's gone.

Sam, Catlin, Michael, and I are all exhausted, but we go to the funeral. How can we not go?

They've found a little place up against a stone wall. They have Doc laid out there on a bed of leaves. They have a freshly dug hole next to him.

Running Bird nods solemnly when he sees us. Dylan pretends not to see us. Lauren is up front, along with Dylan's sidekicks. Everyone walks in a solemn line past Doc, paying their last respects. It's strange; no one is crying, yet I can hear weeping all around me.

When we get close, Dylan moves between us and the body.

"If you're so powerful," he says, "why couldn't you stop him from dying? Why couldn't you stop the aliens from finding us?"

It doesn't feel like he's lashing out because of grief. It feels more calculated than that, more like a performance. As soon as I think this, I feel guilty. Doc was his father. I know what it's like to lose a father.

I just want to say good-bye to Doc, I tell him. *I'm sorry. I'm very sorry.*

"We can't fight them," Dylan says loudly, looking all around. "All we can do is run. You can see how it is. They will kill us all eventually.

"My father gave his life for New America," he continues. "And I will do the same. He would have wanted me to serve New America, and I will."

There's some grumbling that this is not the time to talk of such things, but mostly there's silence. Then others get up to say words about Doc, Robert Penderson among them. Running Bird is the last to go. He sings a death song and talks about how Doc is still alive in many moments and they should all remember this. No one truly dies. "I will especially remember the moments when I beat Lorenzo in chess, which were few but good ones." And then all the words are said and Doc's body is lowered into the grave and that's all. And it doesn't seem enough. It doesn't seem nearly enough.

I seek out Running Bird after the funeral. He welcomes me into his tent, which is once again set apart from the rest of the camp. He tells me about getting my message and putting out the warning to the camp. Thanks to Doc, they had an evacuation plan. The storage cave had a hidden exit to the other side of the mountain. They hid inside the cave while the aliens searched the area. Doc was still alive at this point, though he wasn't conscious—he would never regain consciousness, as it turned out—but he was still alive enough that Running Bird was able to join with him and create a shield over the cave.

"Don't know how he did it," Running Bird says. "Somehow he kept himself alive long enough to get us out of there."

"You and Doc saved them," I say.

Because of you, he mindspeaks. *You must feel the Warrior Spirit now.*

I say maybe. He says that without Doc, New America may not hold together. They need the Warrior Spirit.

"We need you, Warrior Boy."

When I come out of Running Bird's tent, I see Catlin. She looks as tired as I feel, but I appreciate that she's stayed up waiting for me.

"Can you two do a cloak over the camp?" Running Bird says, poking his head out of the tent. "Don't know if I have the strength to do it. I can help if you need me."

We say we can make one. We do, but it's not one of our best efforts. I hope it's good enough.

We make our way to the new supply area to get sleeping bags and then head off in search of a nice spot to lay them down. The sun is out and bright and warm but not hot. We agree that a shady tree would be the best sleeping spot. We look for a good one that's a little off from the main gathering of people.

"I know you just want to sleep," Catlin says. "I do, too. But I need to ask you about something."

I point to a tree that has a nice pocket of shade and some grassy weeds underneath it. She nods.

"What's wrong?"

She looks around like she's afraid someone might be listening. "I felt something strange when I walked by Doc's body," she says. "Like there was something altered in him."

"Altered how?" I ask.

"I don't know," she says. "He just felt different."

"Well, he's, you know, dead," I point out. I know. Snarky. Tired.

"I think we should talk to Marta. Something wasn't right about Doc."

"Okay," I say. "We can talk to her. I've got to rest first, though."

"Rest first," she agrees.

We lie down in the grass, so tired we hardly manage to lay out our bags.

"Just rest our eyes," I say. "Maybe just rest our eyes for a minute, and then we'll talk to her."

"Just for a minute," she agrees.

«««((34)»»»

I wake up to the sound of giggling. I open my eyes and see two girls looking down at me and Catlin. We have our arms wrapped around each other. Catlin is still asleep. The girls giggle some more when they see that I'm awake, see me become aware of how tangled my body is with Catlin's.

"Go away," I whisper to the girls.

That really ups the giggling. They run off.

Catlin wakes up, sleepy eyed. She almost smiles with her almost smile. She yawns prettily, stretching her thin brown arms.

"What time is it?" she asks.

Then she hears the girls giggling from a little distance.

"What's that?" she says.

"Girls," I say. "They saw we were sleeping tangled together."

"Sorry," she says, pulling away and blushing.

"No reason to be sorry," I say, already missing her warmth.

Just then, an alien ship passes overhead. It banks and goes right, and it reminds me once again that I'm not free.

"They're getting closer," I say. "They know we're near."

We work on strengthening the cloak we put over the camp earlier. It's not powerful enough, though. Not for the long term. And now Doc is gone. He always knew what to do. Like my father. I miss him—I miss them both. And now there's an empty place in New America. I feel it, and everyone else feels it. And I feel something else: a lot of people are depending on me to fill it.

"They're too close," I say. "You know they are. They'll find us eventually."

"Maybe," Catlin says.

This irritates me. Maybe? No maybe. I'm tired of pretending. Even if I do have the Warrior Spirit in me— and that's still an "if" as far as I'm concerned—it wasn't enough to stop them from finding us. And it won't be enough to save the rest of us.

And Doc is dead. He held us together. What's going to hold us together now? I'm so sick of losing people. Losing everyone.

"We can't get far enough away, Catlin. That's the truth. Stay or hide in caves, they'll find us eventually. It's all just putting off the inevitable. I don't know why I thought the rebel camp would be any different. I was fooling myself."

Catlin looks awake now. "What's this all about, Jesse?"

"What do you think it's about?" I snap.

"I don't know," she says reasonably. "That's why I asked."

"People just keep dying," I say. "The aliens are too strong, and there are too many of them. It's time we faced that."

"You're wrong."

"We can't win. It comes down to that."

"You forget that we're changing," Catlin says. "We're getting stronger. It means something. And you—you can do things no talented person has ever been able to do. I believe you're chosen to get us through this. I have faith in you."

Her cheeks are flushed with color.

"I didn't ask for your faith," I snap. "I don't want it."

She looks like I've just strangled her puppy. What did she expect? She's a fool to put her faith in me. They all are.

She reaches out to touch me, and I take a step back.

"You're stupid," I say. "We are going to die, and there's nothing anyone can do about it. Least of all me."

She turns her back on me and walks off. Then she starts to run. I know from the shiver down her back, from the way her head bows, that she's crying.

"Catlin!" I shout.

But she doesn't stop.

"I didn't mean—"

I did, though. I meant everything I just said.

I don't run after her. I go the opposite way instead, into the thick trees and away from the trail. I climb. Just like I did that first morning in the old camp. The sun drops below a peak to the west, and the temperature starts to drop. I keep climbing.

My dad tries to talk to me. He appears on the trail in front of me. "Are you really going to run from your problems?" He sounds disappointed. I don't let him say any more. I make him go away. I think how I don't believe in him, not really, and as soon as I think this, he's gone.

I don't believe in anything. I don't believe in the Warrior Spirit. I don't believe we can fight and win. I don't believe we can even survive. I've been pretending. I've just been fooling myself.

I struggle up a rocky slope. I stumble a few times on the loose rocks, but I keep going. I think I might just climb all the way to the top of this mountain. It's the kind of useless act I'm totally used to.

It's all useless. The end is the same no matter what we do. We die. What's the point?

At the top of the slope, I have to rest to catch my breath. In the fading light, I see something move. It's not small. And not alone. Two other shapes are with it. I brace myself for a fight.

I move a few steps closer and accidentally kick a rock. It clatters down the mountain in the still evening air.

Three surprised brown and black faces turn toward me. A deer and her two fawns.

They're beautiful.

How can they be here? Fawns.

They stare at me for what seems like minutes but is probably only seconds, and then the mother turns and runs and the fawns follow.

How?

I collapse onto the loose rocks, which poke into my backside.

How is it possible they're here? They were all killed.

But then I realize that of course it's possible. That's life. The aliens didn't kill off all life. The deer found each other, and now there are fawns that will eventually have fawns of their own. It's life doing what life does.

I'm the stupid one. I'm letting them take my life now without a fight. I'm giving up. I won't do that. I won't give them my life. They will have to fight me for it.

《《《《(35)》》》》

I hurry down the mountain. I've walked a long way, though, and while it's easier going down, it's still not easy. There's no trail. I slip and fall once and skin my hand and arm. The twilight gives way to darkness as I get to the tree line. Then it's trees and bushes and under-growth. I worry that I might be lost, but I tell myself I'm not. I keep going. Eventually I find a narrow trail that twists its way to the main trail, which leads to a place they've set up for eating. One of the cooks is gathering little packages of chips that I recognize from our raid on Taos.

"Have you seen Catlin?" I ask.

"Town meeting," he says. "Down the path a little ways. Deciding whether we stay or go. I say it don't mat-ter either way."

"You're wrong," I say. "It does matter."

"It does?" He looks at me uncertainly.

"Yes."

"Okay," he says. "You better get down there, then."

I hurry to the little clearing they're using to meet. I see Catlin in the crowd next to Zelda and Zack and Sam and Michael, feel her more than see her. Can she see me? I try to send her a telepathic message, just her, a wall-to-wall type message: *I'm sorry I'm so stupid.*

Several rebels look up, so I guess I didn't do a very good job of making it one-to-one. Then I think maybe that's not so bad because I owe everyone an apology. I think it again, and this time I don't try to limit it to Catlin and I hear it like a loud shout that spreads out over the valley, like an echo. *I'm sorry I'm so stupid!* Confused faces turn toward me.

"We can live," I say to the man and woman next to me. He is tall, and she is short.

"I thought we *were* living," she says.

"I've always been under that impression," the man says.

"No, I mean *live* live."

"What did I mean?" the short woman asks the tall man.

"Darned if I know what the difference is between live and live live. You look alive to me, honey."

"Thank you, sweetie," she says.

"You have something to say?" Running Bird says to me from up front.

"Just that you're right, Catlin. I didn't see it, but you are totally right. We can live."

"That's right," Dylan says, standing. "We can live. If we go to the caves right now, we can live."

"We can't hide in the caves," I say. "I've seen the future."

Dylan smiles in a condescending way. "You've been hanging with Running Bird too long. You're beginning to sound like him."

He gets a few more laughs than I'd like.

"I admit I don't know for sure what we need to do next, but I do know you're not the right choice."

His smile fades. "The people have decided I am. I'm going to lead them to Mexico. You're not invited."

"This has not been decided," Running Bird says.

I can see that Dylan's friends are spread out in the crowd, talking to people. They're calling in favors. They're saying it was Doc's last wish that Dylan lead. They're using everything they can so that when they call the vote Dylan will win. Maybe he will. That will be that.

But I can't let that be that.

"You're going to keep people safe?" I say. "Like you had Marta keep Doc safe?"

It's a guess, but not a wild one. I remember what

I saw my first day in camp—Dylan whispering over Doc—and how Marta wouldn't let Catlin see Doc and how Dylan was performing at the funeral and how much he wants to be in charge, and each thing by itself maybe isn't much but all together they mean something. What they mean is almost too awful to believe, but I do.

Everyone looks at Marta, who is up front near Running Bird and Dylan and next to Lauren and some of Dylan's friends. Her daughter is next to her.

"I don't know what he means," she says.

I can feel her pulse quicken, see the way she looks beyond everyone, and I know.

"Yes, you do," Catlin says.

"Crazy talk," Marta says to everyone. "I don't know anything."

She sounds convincing. She really does. Then Marta's daughter mindspeaks, *You need to tell them, Mom.* I think she says this just to Marta, but I can hear it.

Shut up, girl, Marta says. *You shut your mouth.*

"I won't shut up," the girl says out loud. "I've shut up for too long."

"Take Marta and her daughter out of here," Dylan says to one of his friends. "When New Bloods turn mothers and daughters against each other, we've got to do something."

"Mom," the girl says, "tell them what he made you do!"

One of Dylan's friends grabs the daughter by the wrist. "Come on, girl."

"Let go of her!" Marta shouts. She turns back toward Dylan, and she looks scared. She looks like she would run if she could, but the crowd has closed around her.

"He talked me into it," Marta says. "It was just supposed to make Doc sick long enough for Dylan to get what he wanted. I believed him. We need to hide. I want my daughter to be safe. We'll never be safe here. But Dylan increased the dosage after the last town meeting. He couldn't risk Doc's getting better."

People look at Dylan. I go into the past, which was the future the first time I saw the image—Dylan looking down at Doc on the cot. He's trying to pretend he's sad, but actually he's happy. Dylan forces something down Doc's throat. He says, "Good-bye, old man."

"She's lying," Dylan says now. "Can't you see? They're both lying. They're in with the New Bloods."

"I should have been stronger," Marta says with a sob.

The crowd is silent. None of their usual murmuring and chattering. Shock, I guess. But something is building. I can feel it.

"Stupid," Dylan says, and a protective shield goes up around him as he pulls a gun. The element of surprise. Dylan has it.

He swings the gun around and orders his friends to follow him. Then he backs away from the crowd and orders one of his friends to bring the healer.

"We'll need her," he says.

I feel time stop. Everything freezes except me. I run toward Dylan, pushing aside the still forms of people as gently as I can. I don't know how much time I have, but I need to get the gun before Dylan gets away. And I almost make it. Almost. But I'm still a good two feet away when time starts back up again and Dylan doesn't hesitate; he aims his gun and fires at me.

(((((36)))))

A lot of things happen at once. The roar of the crowd starts back up. Dylan's bullet comes at me. And I step out of the moment.

I move to another moment. In that one I fall, dying.

Wrong moment.

I move into another. In that one I've turned so the bullet enters my side. Hurts. Maybe I'll live, maybe not. Catlin rushes toward me, her expression horrified.

Wrong moment.

There are a lot of variations of these moments. I die, and I die, and I may or may not die, but I fall and am helpless in all of these. But then I find one where I don't. Just one.

In that moment, the moment in which I live, I raise my hand and use my mind to turn the bullet. And the bullet misses me. I choose that moment. I step back into it; the bullet misses me.

But Dylan is not done with me yet. He takes aim again, and neither of us sees Lauren until it's too late. She rushes between Dylan and me just as a second shot goes off. She stops so suddenly. I can hear the surprised breath catch in her throat. I will hear it for the rest of my life.

I try to force myself backward, back to an earlier moment, so I can stop Lauren from jumping between us, but I can't. I can't force myself anywhere. I'm stuck in this terrible moment, one of the worst in many terrible moments since the aliens invaded.

Lauren falls.

Catlin gets to Lauren before I do and tries to pull her back from death, but I can feel Lauren going, slipping away, and I know even Catlin can't help her.

I try talking to the Warrior Spirit even though I don't even know if he's there. I beg him to save her. I say if he's a god and he's really in me, then he will. Silence.

I kneel by Lauren. I take her hand. She says something, but her voice is gone. I lean close to her and mind-whisper, *You'll be okay. You're going to be fine.*

Liar. I can pick them, can't I? A boy who's in love with another girl and a boy who's in love with himself.

I want to say something that will make things better, but it's too late for that. All I can do is kiss her on the cheek, a hopeless gesture that is too little and much too late. I almost loved her. Sometimes *almost* is an unforgivable word. You might as well say you were drowning and were almost saved.

I guess I won't be the first woman president after all, she mindspeaks.

I smile. She smiles. It's her real smile, her private one. And for a second it's almost all right, and in another second she's gone.

(((((37)))))

I look up and see Catlin and Michael staring helplessly at Lauren. Another dead — and this time Lauren. Lauren.

I stand, scanning for Dylan. I'm going to kill him. I'm going to make the world a better place.

"Where'd he go?" I say to no one in particular.

Michael looks around and sees what I see — no Dylan.

"Gone," he says.

"I don't see Running Bird, either," Catlin says.

I'm about to take off running, though I don't know which direction to run in. But I don't get a chance.

I hear them before I see them. Not Dylan. Not his sidekicks. Too powerful. A second later the killing begins.

Sorry for your loss.

Sorry for your loss.

Sorry for your loss.

It's chaos. People are trying to run away, but in their panic, they run into one another. I'm yelling with my mind for them to fight the way we've trained. I'm yelling at them to form groups, to join. The Hunter hears me. He smiles when he catches sight of me in the crowd.

There you are! he thinks, like we're old friends. *So nice to see you again.*

I manage to get a group of three—two women and one man—to join. And Catlin and I join. And we attack. We attack the group of hunters that have made a little wedge into our camp, like an arrowhead, with *the* Hunter at the front.

Surprise. The aliens are surprised by our strength and even more surprised when they're shot. I look up the hill and see Running Bird and Michael firing rifles from between the trees. The aliens see them, too, and stop the next round of bullets in midair. Running Bird and Michael have automatic rifles, though, and they keep firing, faster than the aliens can stop the bullets. I see a hunter drop.

I can feel that the Hunter is furious about the guns. He thinks of the guns as machines. He has the alien hatred of anything machine.

Catlin and I kill a hunter who's distracted by the bullets. The Hunter comes toward us then. He sends some kind of wave that knocks Michael and Running Bird back. I don't know if it kills them or just knocks them off their feet, and I don't have time to check because the Hunter is headed straight for me.

He mindspeaks, *Time to die. Past time to die, Dream-walker.*

People are backing away, trying to retreat without full-out running. The Hunter's focus on me takes it off them, and many make it to the safety of trees. The hunters chase after them in their awkward alien way but can't keep up. They may be awesome fighters, but they run like ducks.

Nearly everyone has made it to the trees. It's just me and Catlin now, holding our ground. The other hunters have closed around us; we're surrounded.

Some movement from up the hill catches my eye. Michael and Running Bird are running down the hill toward us. I'm so relieved to see that they're alive that it takes me a second to realize they're headed for certain death. I mindshout at them to run away, but they don't.

The Hunter stands before me. *You're keeping everyone waiting.*

I need to make this stop. I try to freeze time again or move into another moment. Something. *Anything.*

And then . . . I'm gone.

I'm on the peak of a mountain, though not the one I climbed earlier. There's mist all around, through which

I can just see a valley below and other mountains, all thick with trees.

Where in the devil's home am I?

Off to my right is one of those tall book stands. A book is open on top of it, the pages flipping in the soft wind.

"It is all written," says a voice from the wind.

"Are you the Warrior Spirit?" I ask, though who else can it be, really? "If you are, you're a crappy god. You didn't help me when I asked. You didn't save Lauren."

"It was written that she would die," the voice says. "Is written, will be written. And I am not the Spirit of the Warrior."

"Who are you, then?"

But the wind voice ignores my question. "*You* are the Spirit of the Warrior. Well, technically, the Spirit is within you. Read the book. All questions and all answers are contained in its pages."

"My friends—"

"They are safe—for now. Read the book. Read the book and know."

I walk over to the book, wondering if any of this is really happening or if the Hunter killed me and this is some joke. Like maybe the angels and god or gods play this joke on everyone—look at that guy believing he's really getting to read *the* book!

The pages keep blowing one way and then the other.

I put my hands on them to hold them in place. I try to read a few lines, but the words won't stay in place. They fade and come into focus and fade again. I think they even change.

"Everything is written, was written, and will be written," the wind voice says. "But it is not written in stone."

I can't focus. I force myself to concentrate. One line catches my eye. Just one. But I think the wind, whatever the wind is, means for me to see that one line.

"That is my gift," the wind says.

"Nothing is written in stone," I say because I feel like I almost understand. Then I think I do. "Nothing is written in stone, but everything is written."

I don't have a lot of time to think this over. I'm back in my moment. The Hunter, swollen with power and rage, is right in front of me. Catlin, Michael, Running Bird, and I are surrounded and completely outnumbered.

In this moment and in this place, we are about to die. It's written. So, we can't be in this moment and this place.

"Explain to me how we got here again," Michael says.

We're sitting on a cliff above the camp: me, Michael, Catlin, and Running Bird. But just a few moments ago, we were standing in the center of camp, surrounded by aliens.

"I saw it in my mind. Then I thought of us here. And here we are."

"But how?" Michael says.

"I read it in THE BOOK," I say.

"What book?" Michael says.

"THE BOOK."

"That really clears things up," Michael says.

I describe it, then I say, "There was a sentence in it that said the four of us could move from the place of death to this place, but I would have to see it. Then the book showed me. I saw it was one in billions of possibilities—the only one we weren't dead in. I only saw it because I saw it in the book. I couldn't have found it on my own. I pictured this place in my mind the second I got back to the place of death, and we were there, and then we were here."

"But *how?*" Michael says again. "I'm not complaining—I'd rather be here than dead—but how could we be there one second and here the next?"

"All is written," Running Bird says, "but it is not for us to know the whole story. We are a few lines, nothing more."

"But not written in stone," I say.

Running Bird looks disturbed but thoughtful and, for once, has nothing to say. Michael looks more irritated than thoughtful.

I look over at Catlin, who has been unusually quiet this whole time. Even in the dim light, I can feel her eyes locking on to mine.

There's no talent for what you just did. None of the talented have ever done something like that, she mindspeaks at me. *You have the spirit in you.*

You still have faith in me?

Yes.

I have faith in you, I mindspeak.

She smiles. I wonder if she knows what I mean. There's no doubt. There's no almost.

· · • ● • · ·

We lost some moments somewhere. Maybe hours. We realize this as we make our way down the mountain. We go to the clearing about a mile off, where Running Bird—wisely, it turned out—ordered everyone to meet in case of another attack. We're relieved to see a lot of New Americans there. Some are asleep, some awake. They gather around us, thanking the gods that we're safe.

Running Bird asks how many were lost in the attack, and they tell us twenty-three were killed or are missing. Twenty-three.

Also missing are Dylan and his friends, who ran off during the confusion. "Good riddance," most people say—but not all.

Some people say that they want to make a stand here or go back to our first camp, our home, and make a stand there. They want to fight.

"They're too strong," I argue. "We barely got away this time. We were lucky. Any stand will be a last stand."

"So what do we do?" someone asks. "We can't run. We can't fight. What else is left?"

"We need the Warrior Spirit's third way," Running Bird says.

There's some crowd noise, some discussion about what I do and don't know.

"There is a third way," I say. "We have to put distance between us and the aliens now. That's the first thing we have to do."

That all you got? Running Bird mindspeaks only to me. *Need to be more theatrical and mystical, Warrior Boy. Need to give the people a show. You're going to have to work on that.*

Running Bird says we'll go south to Santa Fe after we bury the dead and pack up what we need. It's about seventy miles through the mountains. We'll be safer there.

I volunteer to go back for the truck, but Running Bird says the aliens will be guarding the vehicles and the road. We need to travel through the forested mountains.

We bury the dead, and Running Bird says words over them. I hear people thinking that this is where we all will end up. I hear them feel more loss and pain.

After the funeral, Running Bird tells us all to rest while the scouts make sure the way south is clear. Michael, Catlin, and I find a spot in the woods away from the others. I lie beside Catlin, suddenly feeling shy. Michael isn't far away, and he begins to snore. He is excellent at snoring, and Catlin and I start giggling. And then we aren't giggling. We're kissing. Kissing and joining. Pleasant as this is, we're both exhausted, and after a while we're content just to hold each other and fall asleep.

And then I dream.

And then I dreamwalk.

Big surprise.

《《《《((39))》》》》》

It would be kind of nice if I could just sleep for once, but I guess that isn't in the Big Book for me. Not now. I have to walk in the dreamworld. I feel I'm looking for something. Maybe the third way.

But it's not the third way I find. At least, I don't think it is. It feels like another moment, a distant moment.

"You see?" Catlin says. "It looks good."

She's showing me a room in a house, pointing out the way the new couch looks. I don't know how I know it's a new couch, but I do. Catlin's older—years older—and I know somehow that I am, too.

A little girl comes running into the room, and I know it's our little girl. I've got a little girl. I can't believe it. I look at the wall where I know I keep the calendar from Betty. August 17, ten years from now. Ten years — but how?

"Daddy and I are talking, Cat," Catlin says to the little girl.

Cat. That's our name for her. I know this. She's four.

"I know," she says. "Daddy should play with me, though."

I look at her, and I can't believe it. I can't believe she's mine. She's perfect.

"What's wrong with Daddy?" Cat says.

I'm crying. I didn't even realize it. "Allergies, Cat," I say, stroking her head.

And the moment is gone. I'm back lying next to Catlin. But it is a moment, a moment of our future. But that's not exactly right. It's a moment of a possible future.

Catlin and Michael are still asleep, and I sneak away quietly and go look for Running Bird. I ask Zack, who is eating some canned peaches he's saved, if he's seen him.

"He's just sitting on a rock. He looks like a statue. People are getting kind of worried."

"Running Bird has his own way."

"You can say that again."

And I can't resist because I'll take the easy ones. "Running Bird has his own way."

"Ha, ha," he says. But he smiles, and I feel a slight

lightening of his mood. Worth the effort. Totally worth it.

Zack wants to go with me, but I say I need to talk to Running Bird privately.

Running Bird is, as Zack said, sitting cross-legged on a rock, so still he might be a statue. With that stomach he does look a little like Buddha—well, a Hispanic, white, African-American, Native American Buddha.

"Running Bird," I say when I get close. "Can I talk to you?"

"Don't know," he says. "Can you?"

He sounds so much like my mother, the English teacher, that I think he's channeling her for a second.

"I saw a future," I say.

"No such thing," he says.

"Okay, a now. But a now that's ten years away from this now."

"And what did you see in this moment?"

"Catlin and I had a little girl."

"That's interesting," he says.

"Interesting?" I repeat. "It's more than interesting! It means that we have a future on that time line. We as in humans. It's years from now—ten years, at least. We have a future."

"So there is a third way," Running Bird says.

"That's what I'm saying," I say. "There must be for that future to exist. But what is it? How do we get there?"

"You lead us," he says.

"I don't know how," I say.

"Maybe the answer isn't to go forward. Maybe it's to go backward."

"You mean . . . ? Wait, what do you mean?"

"Don't try to figure out how to get there. Try to figure out how to get back here *from* there. Work your way back to this moment, and you'll see how you got there."

The thing about Running Bird is that for all his irritating habits and all his double-talk, he knows things. You could even say he's wise in a twisted kind of way.

"That's all, huh?"

"You want to save the human race, you better get walking."

"What are you going to do?"

"Sit here. Nice view."

Actually, it isn't. There are a lot of nice views in these mountains, but this isn't one of them.

"This isn't a nice view," I say.

"Can be if you know how to look."

I look at him closely. "You're messing with me, aren't you?"

"You're the Chosen One. You should know."

Yeah, he's back to just plain irritating.

(((((40)))))

The scouts return, Zelda among them, and we gather in the clearing and divvy up the supplies. We do it as quickly as we can, but it takes a while because of the large number of people.

The old woman who complained about the snorer at that first town meeting gets her food. Then I notice who she's with. It's the snorer. She sees me notice.

"What?" she says. "I can't have a boyfriend?"

"I just thought you didn't like each other."

"I mostly just use him for sex," she says, and an image I seriously hope to never see again pops into my mind.

And then something else happens. She smiles. And it's a beautiful smile. It really is.

And this little surprise feels big. It makes me smile.

And then I feel it, a slight dizziness, and then I've moved forward. I've moved to another place in time, but I'm here, too, at the same time. I'm in two places at once again.

Catlin gives me her almost smile from the passenger seat. We're driving up MoPac into Austin. There's a baby in the backseat in one of those car seats. Cat, I guess. I'm really nervous suddenly. What if I hit a bump? What if a squirrel runs in front of the car and I veer off the road without thinking?

Catlin's blond hair is long. It goes all the way down her back.

"I'm glad we came back," she says.

We're listening to the radio. It's a report. The government of New America, led by President Johnson, is having troubles. There's a revolt in New New England, which I somehow know is a state now, and gangs of renegades in the New South and New Texas still control whole cities. I know these troubles have been going on for a long time.

Six states, I think. There are six big states now, and the government of New America is far too small to exert any real control over the states.

We come to a checkpoint with soldiers. We have to show papers. The soldiers direct us to a building where we have to register in order to stay in the city. This is how it is now. The city is "protected" by the soldiers, but anything outside of the city walls is not protected.

"She's waking up," Catlin says.

I look over my shoulder, and I see Cat's eyes opening. I'm a father. How can I be a father? I can't even take care of myself. She smiles at me. The baby smiles at me, and I know I am a father because my heart fills up with that smile. Nothing gets by it. Not the threats. Not the killings. Not the rumors of a new leader in New Texas heading this way whose powers are so strong that gangs of renegades are uniting behind him. All these things I know about, but none of them can get through that smile.

"Jesse?" Catlin says.

I blink at her. She looks so young. And yet the same, too. "Hey."

"Hey, yourself. You went somewhere just then, didn't you?"

I nod. Somewhere. I can see the future because it's now. I've always been able to see the past, like everyone. We're all time travelers in that way. But I can go forward, too. And when I go, I'm there, really there, and here. It's a lot to accept.

But if I do accept it — accept it and the possibilities of different futures — I see a universe full of choices.

"Where'd you go?"

I wonder if I should tell her. After all, she has just as much right to know about our future as I do. But what if telling her keeps it from happening somehow? I mean, we just kissed for like the first time. If this was the old world, this would be the time to ask her out to a movie or dinner or something. I sure wouldn't be talking about our future kid.

It's not the old world, though.

And we're alive in the future. At least in that future. That is something pretty amazing. So I do tell her. I tell her everything.

It's afternoon before we set out. The forest thickens and thins, and we go up and down hills and mountains. Sometimes we walk along a highway that winds through the country and sometimes through the forest. Running Bird seems to know this area well — well enough to guide us in the moonlight, because it isn't long before we're walking in the dark. Eventually we come to a stream, and Running Bird says this is a good place to stop for the night.

They're waiting for us. They make sure we're all at the stream or near it before they attack. I feel them before the others do, but not soon enough. They're already killing before I can warn anyone.

I shout for people to join and raise shields. I feel the power of the aliens like an electric current rushing through the air. The hunters have that same wedge as before. *They knew we were coming here,* I think. *There's no other explanation for how they're here.* But there's no time to think this over. There's only acting and reacting.

I hear someone next to me say, *"Madre!"* right before he falls.

A wave of people die right in front of me.

Join! I mindshout. *Defensive moves! Join! Defensive moves!*

Some people do join. Some people do attempt some of the defensive moves we've worked on. Catlin and I create a shield that the hunters punch right through, but it slows them down a little. We create another, and another. We fight back. I see now that this is not the main group of hunters; there are only about ten of them. The Hunter is not among them.

Catlin and I kill one. The aliens kill three more of us. They're strong and fast. Too fast. Too strong.

I unjoin from Catlin. I do something then. I don't even know how I know to do it, but I do. I create some kind of wave, control some kind of energy that hits them hard enough some of them fall back. And I feel it. They're confused. A few of them are afraid. They hesitate. That's when I realize that their commanding officer is dead.

"Retreat!" I shout. *Fall back!*

We retreat, but it's not an orderly retreat. People scatter. The hunters call for reinforcements, but they don't try to follow us. They hold their position, trying to kill whoever is within their range.

We run through the woods. The darkness gives us cover but also makes running difficult, even dangerous. A lot of people fall. One woman has to be carried after spraining or breaking her ankle.

Eventually we gather at another clearing, this one smaller than the last. We call to each other in the dark. Catlin works on the wounded. Running Bird orders me to post sentries, and then he sends a scout back where we've come from to be sure the aliens aren't following.

"How do they keep finding us?" I say, staying on my feet because I'm too worked up to lie down. I pace. My dad used to pace, and it irritated me and my mom, but here I am pacing just like he did.

No one answers. Catlin is busy working on the wounded. The other rebels are busy trying to catch their breath and grieving for the dead and fighting the feeling of—there's no other word for it—doom. No one has an answer.

Another moment. I go to another moment instead of hearing an answer. I'm dying. The Hunter is standing over me. Running Bird is dead. Michael is dead. Sam is dead. Zelda is dead. Zack is dead. And Catlin, Catlin is dead, too.

You have been worthy prey, he mindspeaks. *I'm sorry for your loss.*

I'm sorry for your loss.

I'm sorry for your loss.

I'm sorry for your loss.

I see variations of my death, but they all end the same way. Everyone I care about is dead, and I'm the last to die—though I do die—I always die, and the Hunter is always saying, *I'm sorry for your loss.* Over and over and over.

I was beginning to believe in the future I'd imagined before, the future with Catlin and me alive together and with Cat. But that is just one version of the future. One of thousands of versions. *I'm sorry for your loss.* Maybe all but one ends with those words. How can I possibly find it?

"He's stabilized," Catlin says.

I nod distractedly. "How do they keep finding us?" I say again.

"I don't know," Catlin says. "Michael doesn't have anything in him, if that's what you're thinking. I've checked him closely."

"Could you have missed something?"

"No," she says, and then she stops. "Unless . . ."

"Unless what?"

"I didn't check you or Zack or myself. I didn't think—"

"Check me," I say.

She finds it almost right away. He didn't even bury it deeply. I just couldn't feel it. I feel her pull it out of me, though, and I also feel a deep shame. Too weak to feel it. Too weak.

"Stupid," she says. "I should have checked us all."

"It's my fault," I say. "They've been tracking us through me."

"You couldn't know."

Because we're weak and they are strong. Just like they've always told us.

She checks herself and Zack. They're both clean.

"Son of a female dog." The Hunter had a contingency plan for his contingency plan. He used me. The son of a female dog used me.

"Put it back," I tell Catlin.

"What?"

"Put it back in me."

"But—" And then she realizes. "You're sure?"

"I'm tired of running," I say.

And she puts it back.

«««((42))»»»

In the morning we go back to where we were attacked. If there are others from our group still out there somewhere, they might gravitate to this position.

There are no aliens at the clearing. I knew there wouldn't be. For whatever reason, the Hunter couldn't make the last ambush. He was probably pretty upset about that. He won't decline the next ambush invitation. He'll be right there at the front, leading. He'll let us gather back together, and then he'll make a special visit.

But it won't be on his terms this time. I join with Catlin, and together we put out a call into the woods, telling any survivors from New America to meet up back at the clearing. We don't even try to hide it. I'm sure the aliens can hear us. In fact, I'm counting on it.

Running Bird comes over from where he's been tending to the wounded and asks me if I'm crazy. "Every alien in a ten-mile radius just heard that call," he says.

They know where we are anyway, I mindspeak just to him. *They've known all along.*

He grabs my arm and leads me off a ways into the woods.

"Tell me," he says.

So I do.

"I should have felt it," I say. I do feel it now. I control it. What it transmits and what it doesn't. But I'm too late.

"We have no time for guilt," he says. "You need to lead us to the future where we survive. That's what you need to do."

I tell him I had Catlin put the tracker back in my brain. I tell him I can control it. Running Bird looks like he wants to argue, but then I feel him change his mind. He decides to trust me. We go back to the clearing and find Sam and have a meeting.

Sam listens and even seems to agree about the element of surprise and how much of an advantage it is.

"We need to be ready," I say. "We need to use guns. They're good distractions. The aliens come in like a wedge every time, don't they? They're predictable. How can we use that against them?"

Sam devises a plan.

Is it a good plan? I'm no military person. I don't know. I do know that this is a place, a moment, that's very important on the line. There are a whole lot of possible bad moments beyond our fight with the Hunter. Thousands. More, probably. But I know there's at least one good one. And I have to believe there's a way to get there. I have to.

43

We tell everyone that we will be attacked again. The news goes over better than I thought it would. Most New Americans don't panic. Everyone is scared, but there's a kind of relief in finally making a stand against the aliens.

We practice scenarios of the attack and defensive moves and counterattacks. We drill. And then we drill some more. Zack is happy, and even Zelda seems to accept that this is the time to fight.

When we walk on toward Santa Fe, Running Bird and I are at the front of the New Americans, Sam and Michael and Catlin at the rear. The path is narrow and the woods thick around us for much of the way. Rocky sides of mountains hem us in. If we're caught here on this path, we'll be trapped. Hoping to get to a wider path or a more open area, I try to hurry the others.

We do, eventually, and we're able to slow down, which is good because everyone is tired. We rest and walk and rest and walk the day away. No one attacks. It's near dusk, near time to set up a camp, when we come to a clearing in the woods. Sam suggests that we go to the other side of the clearing and camp there.

We get sloppy as we cross the clearing and lose our lines. Everyone is ready to rest. I order them to re-form the lines, but they're tired and the response is listless and uneven. When I turn back to try to get them to move, the attack starts.

There are two groups of them this time. A smaller group attacks from behind while the main group attacks from ahead, both in their standard wedge formation. I take a small amount of satisfaction from the fact that they think we're dangerous enough to change tactics and make their attack less predictable.

The Hunter is where I knew he'd be, though. He's attacking with the main group, at the point of the wedge. As we practiced, we form two squads. Those in back face the hunters from that direction, and the rest of us face the Hunter and the main force.

Sam's shooters are quickly up into the woods, both north and south, and they fire as the rest of us attack with kicks, punches, and blocks — most of them physical but some of them mental.

We're still outpowered, but our preparedness seems

to catch the aliens by surprise. The shooters do exactly what they're supposed to do. They draw the aliens' attention, weakening their focus.

Sensing the weakness, we attack harder. I send my wave of whatever at them, which disrupts their defense long enough for a few bullets to get through. One of the aliens is hit and spins back into others. But more of our people die.

I'm sorry for your loss.

The Hunter gets close to me then. He lets the others worry about the bullets. He thinks that I am the key. I think that he is. He does something that knocks me to the ground and that I have no defense for. That's when I see it again. The future. One of a thousand moments when we are all dead. A million. Me first. He says, *Sorry for your loss.*

I see it. I'm in it.

I try to push him away, break his hold, but it's like I'm being strangled. I can't break the grip of his hands. This is the moment of my death. Deathgiver. He was right.

Sorry for your loss.

Catlin joins with me. I try to break from her because if she joins, then she'll fall, too. She will die, too. Even together, we aren't strong enough to break his hold. All she's done is made it easier for him to kill us both.

Then I feel something else. Something on the

Hunter. I'm able to move my head enough to see. It's Running Bird. He's jumped on the Hunter's back. *"No!"* I cry, because I know what happens next; I've seen it. Wile E. Coyote blows up the Road Runner. That TNT in the road finally gets him.

I see Running Bird explode, see the Hunter make him split apart.

Catlin's screams are echoing in my head, and it's all happening just as I've seen it. The Hunter is reaching out to split Catlin apart, like he's done a thousand times, and as she falls, I do to him what I did to that rock Running Bird threw at me what seems like a century ago: I split him. He's split into pieces. They fly off in all directions.

That stupid nursery rhyme comes to my mind: "All the kings horses and all the king's men . . ."

But I'm wrong.

He's so powerful that he pulls the pieces back together; they rejoin. He's so powerful that the life flows back into him. He even begins to smile. But then he looks down. Catlin stands before him, and she's holding one small piece of him in her hand. She crushes it.

His smile fades. It's been a long time since he's been surprised. That's what he thinks. Then he crumbles, and the pieces of him shatter on the ground.

And he dies, his body next to Running Bird's.

· · · • · ·

When the other hunters feel their leader die, they can't believe it at first. Then I feel it in them. Fear. Confusion and fear. This time, they're the ones who run. This time we hold our ground. There's cheering, but I don't cheer. I kneel by Running Bird. Catlin kneels and tries something, but she knows it's useless. We saw him break inside.

She pulls on my arm. "There'll be more of them coming."

"Probably," I say, still kneeling by his body.

"We've got to go."

Zack and Zelda tell Catlin a girl's hurt over by the trees. Catlin goes into my mind and takes the tracking device out of me and then runs. Zack stays behind me and looks down at Running Bird.

"He's old," Zack says. "You wouldn't think he'd be so strong."

"No."

"He was, though."

"Yeah, he was."

"I killed one of them," Zack says. "With a gun."

"You did good," I say.

"It doesn't feel good," Zack says. "I thought it would."

"No," I say.

"I really thought it would."

"I know," I say, still looking at Running Bird. And

then I say, "We don't have any choice, Zack. They haven't left us any choice."

It's a soldier's thing to say, I guess. I never wanted to be a soldier. Doesn't matter.

"I know," he says, and looks embarrassed. He starts walking off.

"Zack," I say, and he stops and looks back at me. "It's good that it doesn't feel good."

He stares at me for a second, then says, "Yeah," and walks on.

Sam comes over and says we need to go. We need to move on and find a place to sleep. So we move on — just like we've had to do and have to do, leaving the dead behind.

44

We walk back into the forest. We stumble along for a couple of hours, the chill of the night taking hold of the air, and then we sleep on a damp hillside beneath thick pines. There's a lot of troubled dreaming and the sounds that come from it, and I wake once to one child crying and another screaming from a nightmare. I get up and walk around because of the noise and the sense that we're being watched, but all I find is a raccoon. I lie back down, and before long I've fallen asleep. Running Bird comes to me in my dream.

"Guess you were right," he says. "The Road Runner was killed after all."

"I wasn't right. Remember? You're still alive in plenty of moments."

"True," he says. "I talked to the wind."

"What did it say?"

"Said it wouldn't let me look at the Big Book."

"Sorry. That book is pretty amazing."

"I like books with pictures anyway," he says. "Find your way back from the future. No one can do that but you."

"The Hunter is dead. We've sent a message," I say, but I know from the nightmares, from the number of dead, that we're limping along, the walking wounded.

Running Bird's expression is inscrutable. "It is not enough, Warrior Boy."

"I know," I whisper.

"You have to do more."

"What? What do I need to do?"

"You're the Warrior Boy, got the Warrior Spirit directing you. Best listen."

I wake up listening, trying to hear something in the wind. There are no answers, just the rustle of leaves in the trees, the stirring of tired and dispirited people, the grieving whispers. And something else; the slightest of satisfactions. We're still alive.

We move on toward Santa Fe before the sun's up. We have people with rifles ahead of us, to the side, and behind. We have scouts farther out. We walk all day and into the night, the last part out in wide-open spaces with hills and mountains that glow almost pink as the sun sets. Then, once it's night, billions of stars fill the big sky. We stop when it seems like we can't go on anymore and make camp.

Sam, who's been out ahead of the group, reports that there are houses in the next canyon. She's going to take some scouts and see if she can find a working phone. She wants to try calling some of the other houses. In particular, she wants to try Albuquerque, which had a large Clan of the Wind, House of Jupiter, before the invasion. I think we both know that we need others, though neither of us is willing to admit it.

Michael says he's going with her. She stares him down.

"Why are you so eager to get killed?"

"I'm your man, Sam. It's written in Jesse's Big Book."

Sam turns to me. I shake my head.

"I don't need lovers," she says. "I need fighters."

"I can't be both?" Michael says.

She shakes her head but tells him he can come.

"What should I tell Albuquerque if I reach them?" she asks me, her gaze steady and penetrating.

"We're here," I say. "Tell them we're here. You know what to ask them."

· · ● · ·

When everyone is settled and the sentries are posted, Catlin and I climb away from the others. I tell her about my dream with Running Bird in it.

"That old man is still messing with me," I say.

"You think it's true?" she says. "About death, I mean. We're still living in some moments even after we die?"

"Maybe," I say.

"I'd like to think so," she says.

We talk about the dead. Her father. My mother and father. Friends. Lindsey. Lauren. Running Bird. Doc. In the shadow of this talk, we join. I lose sight of what is me and what is her. We're like one person. One person who is bigger and more powerful than either of us alone. We're two who are also one.

Later that night, I have a dream that is a moment on the time line — the line that leads to our daughter, Cat. Catlin and I are in a room without windows, a room with stone walls. There's a big screen, like a movie screen, taking up most of a wall.

"I have to reset the codes," a voice says. I turn and see the voice belongs to a man with salt-and-pepper hair and a mustache. His uniform shows he's a colonel, like my dad was.

In the next instant, I have the colonel in a choke

hold, a good one with my forearm tight against his neck.

I skip ahead a few moments. The colonel is on the floor, his eyes fixed on the giant screen on the wall.

"You've destroyed us," the colonel chokes out. "You've signed our death warrant!"

I don't understand. There's always so much I don't understand.

(((((45)))))

In the morning, Sam tells me that she was able to make contact with the Albuquerque House of Jupiter.

"Their house has grown in size, combining with the survivors of other houses and a few New Bloods. They have three hundred talented ones now. And their leader has been in contact with some talented in Los Angeles — New Bloods and a mix of several houses, nearly a thousand survivors. There are more of us alive than we thought or than they let us think. The group in Albuquerque is organized differently from New America. They separate military and civilians."

I let this news sink in. It's good news. There are more of us. I'm unsure about the division between military and civilian, but I understand it. Our nonfighters, the children and elderly and those who can't fight, should be somewhere safer. We should be able to protect them better.

"I've told the colonel about the potential alien landing," Sam continues. "And I filled him in on New America's plan to send a clear message to those thirty million would-be settlers. He agrees that this should be the objective of all missions. He's sending out the word as best he can: attack targets now."

"That's good," I say, and I feel a rush of hope. An army. Okay, not much of an army from the sound of it, but an army fighting back. We aren't alone. "That's very good."

"He's willing to let us join him, join his camp, which he's calling the Fourth Infantry of the Southwest. He has two conditions: he commands, and we divide into military and civilians."

"Do you know anything about him?"

"By reputation," she says. "He's a good man. Not an easy man, maybe. Career military."

"What do you think?"

"This is war," she says. "We've fought well and we've survived, but a lot of it's luck. We have children and elderly who should be somewhere safer. It's hard on them, and it makes us less effective. It would give us stability. We'd fight with a military unit. We'd all have a better chance of surviving."

"And we'd be military."

"Is that so bad?"

"I don't know," I say honestly, remembering the guy in my choke hold, the colonel. *You've signed our death warrant.*

I can't trust my dream, though. I can't know if it will even be our future — if it really is a future. And I know we can't survive like we are.

"New America will do what you say," Sam says. "They've elected you leader without casting a single vote. You know what we should do, though."

I know. I don't see much choice, really. I call a meeting and put it before New America. Sam is right. They want to know what I think we should do. They trust me. I've kept them alive, they say. Not true. We've all kept each other alive, except for those we haven't. Too many.

I say we should join the survivors in Albuquerque.

The trip, by foot, takes us four days. We don't run into any more hunters, though I don't know if it's because they can't track us anymore or because they've had to regroup after the loss of the Hunter. We do run into other survivors: a gang of what turn out to be renegades. There are maybe fifteen of them. They look us over, and when they realize how many of us there are and how armed we are, they retreat into the hills.

I remember the future. These gangs will be powerful.

There will be many of them, small groups willing to kill for what other people have. And some of the gangs will join and make larger gangs and eventually small armies. And there will be wars and fighting. I remember the future, the one we survive in, the best one, and it will be hard, too.

When we reach the camp, the colonel—Colonel Hamilton—is there to meet us. I'm upset but not entirely surprised that he's the colonel from my dream. I shield my thoughts so that he can't see my memory of putting him in a choke hold. Even so, his eyes are cold when they meet mine.

Colonel Hamilton makes a short speech welcoming us. Then he wants to talk to Sam and me in his tent. He has a town-hall tent somewhat like Doc's, but the tent isn't open the way Doc's was. The flaps are closed, and there's a guard standing watch.

Colonel Hamilton is a tall man with salt-and-pepper hair and a thick mustache. The two men in the tent with the colonel have shaved heads. One of them is really big, like pro-football-player big, and the other is small, compact, and fidgety. They're two of his captains. There's a table with some maps spread across it and a few chairs.

I can hear our two groups mixing outside the tent. The colonel's group is offering food and water. We've had a long, hot, dusty walk, and I can hear how glad our group is to have arrived. This camp is like a little town, and I can feel the relief in the minds of our people to finally be someplace safer, if not exactly safe.

The colonel wants a report on everything that's happened so far—basically since I arrived at Doc's camp, at New America. Sam and I take turns telling the story, each of us fleshing out different details. When we get to the part about Doc's murder, the colonel frowns.

"Dr. Cabeza was a good man. That was no way for him to die."

When I mention Running Bird's death, though, the colonel says nothing.

"He was a great man," I hear myself saying, which surprises me. "He saved me. He saved a lot of people."

"As you say," the colonel says, but I can feel that he disapproves of Running Bird for some reason. *Not a serious man,* he thinks.

Once he feels he's been sufficiently debriefed, the colonel begins to explain how his unit operates. "The Fourth is a military unit. We've organized a chain of command. Everyone who can fight is part of the Fourth, but there are civilians here and they're part of the Fourth's responsibility. Our mission is to attack the enemy whenever possible and damage them and stay alive. We've had little contact with other units, but we do know there are other units out there. Communication among units is a work in progress, but, however disorganized, there's an army of fighters. Don't doubt that."

"You've had some contact?"

He nods but won't say any more about that. "There are rules," he tells us. "They are posted. There are penalties for not following the rules. They are posted. We have an MP and three officers who act as judges for any disputes or alleged crimes. We're strict but fair. This is not a peacetime army, though. We're at war. I won't pretend otherwise."

He asks if there are any questions.

I shake my head. "No."

"No, sir!" Sam says, and salutes him. It's natural for her. I wonder if I should salute, but I don't.

The colonel dismisses Sam and his two officers but asks me to stay.

When it's just the two of us, he says, "I assume you agree to my condition about command since you're here?"

"I agree, but I'm not a soldier. My father was."

He says he didn't know my father but he's glad to hear I understand the military.

"Doc called us, the survivors, New America. We've voted on decisions. We've tried to make our group a democracy."

"You know it can't be that way in the military. I like the name, though. New America. That's a good name. The civilians can have it, and we'll pay allegiance to it, but right now we're at war. There'll be time later for democracy. There's no time for it now."

"There has to be," I say.

He sits back, frowning a little, his eyes on me. "In war, some freedoms have to be taken away for the good of the whole. Your father was a soldier, so you know this. No true American likes it, but that is the way it is in war." He pauses. "They say you can dreamwalk. Is that true?"

I nod.

"And I can hear in your people that you fight like the aliens. Remarkable. How did that happen?"

I do my best to explain. I tell him about my martial-arts training and the things I've discovered and how my power has grown over time. He eyes me closely, and I can tell he's trying to decide if I'm an asset or a threat. I think he decides that I'm both.

"Every able man and woman is part of the military. Anyone can refuse and face a hearing to determine if there's a good reason for them to receive a deferment. Otherwise they serve in some capacity."

"I'll fight," I say. It's what I've wanted all along. But what I want to know more than anything is if our decision to join the colonel and the Fourth is the one that will lead to the future I've already seen. And that's something I can't know.

"That'll be all, soldier," he says, already turning his attention to some papers on his desk.

46

The next day, I have a training session with Catlin, Zack, and Michael. Gradually, more and more people manage to find their way over to us until there's a large group — and not all New Americans.

Even the colonel comes by to watch for a while. He doesn't say anything, but after the workout, one of his soldiers comes to get me. He says the colonel wants me to stop by his tent.

The soldier tells me how lucky we all are that we found our way to this camp, where there's a real military leader.

"Colonel Hamilton is a good commander. He's built a real community here. A place to fight for."

When we get to the tent, the colonel is sitting at his desk, smoking a cigar. He has me take a seat. He asks if I'll have a hard-boiled egg.

"Excuse me?"

"Hen laid it this morning."

He hands it to me, and I peel it and take a bite.

"Good," I say. "Very good."

It is. It's been a long time since I've had an egg of any kind.

"We have a thriving community here. We'll be self-sufficient before long. We won't need to go scavenging. We've got chickens and twelve micro vegetable and fruit gardens. We've captured deer, and we're breeding a herd. We've got two goats. We're doing a lot of positive things."

"I see that," I say. And it's true; walking around the camp yesterday, I did see that this little camp feels like people have settled in.

"But all that we're doing here could be taken away in a day. I don't have to tell you that."

"No, sir," I agree.

"So you understand why I'd be concerned when a disruptive element comes into my camp."

"Me?"

"You."

"I'm just trying to prepare people to fight."

"I'm hearing from my men that many of your people think you have the Warrior Spirit in you. Then I see you teaching fighting skills without authorization."

"I'm sorry. I didn't know I needed it."

"Everyone has to learn quickly. I realize this is all new to you, but if you break the rules again, there will be consequences. You need to get authorization for everything beyond tying your own shoes. Is that clear?"

"Yes, sir."

"Good. Now I need you to tell me you don't believe in this Warrior Spirit nonsense."

"I don't believe in it," I lie.

"I'm glad to hear that," he says. "We need to make that clear to everyone. There's no Warrior Spirit. There's just us."

"Yes, sir."

"You can be an inspiration to the men and women here. You have certain skills. You will help morale if you fight even half as well as I'm told you do."

"I'll do my best."

"I'm going to need better than your best, son."

He smokes his cigar thoughtfully, but then I notice that he's trying to push past my shield and read me. He's subtle, but I feel him. I strengthen my shield, and I feel him back away.

"Tell you what," he says. "You have authorization to continue your training sessions. Only you'll do them with my sergeant. His name is Haley. He'll coordinate a schedule. We'll post it."

A soldier excuses himself for interrupting when he

steps into the tent. He says Captain Franks is back from scouting. He's ready to make his report.

"I want a written report on your talents," he says to me. "Everything you've used them for. I'd like to have an idea what you can do."

He makes me sound like a machine, like a weapon.

"Yes, sir."

"By tonight," he says.

Colonel Hamilton dismisses me then. He promises me we'll talk more later. I can hardly wait.

I admit I've always struggled with authority, but I don't feel the immediate trust with Colonel Hamilton that I did with Doc. I'm not even sure joining him was the best move. Anyway, it's done now.

I find Catlin in the hospital tent, helping to organize supplies. They've got stuff that I haven't seen since before the invasion, including an EKG machine and an X-ray machine. I'm impressed, but I also can't help thinking that Catlin's never needed a machine to heal. Her talent is that strong.

We step outside the tent, and I tell her about my conversation with the colonel.

She's frowning. "An egg?"

"That's what you focus on? I tell you I'm worried about the colonel, and you're focusing on the egg?"

"You know how long it's been since I've had an egg?"

I can see her trying to remember, but she can't. "Anyway, what is it about him that worries you, exactly?"

I try to put my concerns into words, but nothing I can think to say sounds all that convincing. Maybe I'm not being fair to the colonel. He's career military. He's tough. That's not necessarily bad. Maybe this world needs tough.

I tell Catlin not to worry about it. I tell her I'm just adjusting. I try to believe myself.

We have some free time before dinner. We go for a little walk in the woods. We try to forget everything that has gone on and will go on. We try to be in the moment. It's not a bad moment to be in, the two of us in the woods alone. I kiss her. She kisses me. We have more good moments, a bunch of them all in a row.

47

That night after dinner, Sam, Catlin, and I are called to the colonel's tent, the command center. I'm starting to feel like it's my second home here at the camp.

Colonel Hamilton has his three captains there. He tells us to take a seat.

"We've had some news from other units. There's an increase in activity in the alien security centers. I had scouts investigate up in Santa Fe, and they report the same thing. The aliens seem to be gearing up for something. We think maybe they're going to try some kind of major strike."

"The settlers," I mutter, flashing back to that endless fleet of alien ships. "They must be about to start shipping them down."

"It would seem so." The colonel sits up straighter. "We've been an irritation to them, and now they want to land those settlers and they've decided they need to do something about us. I think they might be changing their strategy. They've decided they need to act now, take the risk of exposure, rather than risk further attacks by us. If that's the case, we might be down to our last chance to stop them."

He looks each of us in the eye: Sam, Catlin, me. He lingers on me.

"A few miles from here is a sensitive target. We've scouted it. A small force of aliens is there, and the enemy has set up some sort of security wall around the perimeter. We need to get through that wall. From your report, Jesse, you and your friends got through such a wall when you escaped from your captors in Austin."

Catlin and I both nod.

"Why is this place the target, sir?" I ask. I can't imagine how getting into any place, no matter how sensitive, could help us right now.

The colonel takes a long drag from his cigar. "The target is a missile facility. A *nuclear* missile facility," he stresses.

"You want us to—" I start to say.

"I'm ordering you to, soldier. We're going to get into that missile facility, and we are going to deliver some hurt on those aliens. For once we are going to take the battle to them."

"You think the missiles can get to their ships?" I feel uneasy. Nuclear weapons. He wants to fire nuclear weapons.

The colonel tosses his cigar on the ground and puts it out with his boot. "Unfortunately, we can't be sure they would make it. And we can't take the risk of being wrong. We need a plan we can be sure of. As I said before, this could be our last chance."

I glance at Catlin and Sam. If they're making sense of this, they're pretty good at hiding it.

"What are you saying, sir?" I ask.

"They love our green earth and our blue skies. It's what makes this planet desirable to them. So we have to take away those things, make them want to settle somewhere else. I've got thirty-six nuclear missiles in my facility—my former command, I should say. Thirty-six. We can hit thirty-six major cities where the aliens have bases. I believe that hitting those thirty-six cities, besides doing major damage to the settlements, will cause a nuclear fall. It will send them packing for good. No more green. No more blue. No more aliens."

Catlin says, "But that would . . . I mean, wouldn't that destroy everything?"

"We're not talking about a nuclear winter," Colonel

Hamilton snaps, clearly frustrated by our reactions. "This would be a carefully orchestrated attack, the effects of which would be strictly limited to a nuclear fall."

He goes on to explain just what this "nuclear fall" would look like. Within a few days, the world would be covered in smoke. It would be so heavy it would block the sun. Temperatures would cool a few important degrees, killing off those lush green plants the aliens love so much. Rainfall would decrease, drying up all but the biggest rivers. Earth wouldn't be destroyed, though. It would be harmed. It would be wounded. But like a wounded soldier, it would heal, and when it did the aliens would be long gone.

"We're talking five or six years, tops," the colonel says. "And the effects might even be less than those I've described. We can survive it. Earth will take a hit, but it will survive, and so will we."

"Bomb our own cities," Catlin says. "Kill everything that's alive? What about the animals and the plants?"

"I don't like it, either," Colonel Hamilton says. "I've thought about this long and hard, and the truth of the matter is that we have no choice. If we don't act now, we won't have a chance. Humankind will cease to exist. We're in a unique position here. This was my missile facility. I know the codes. We've got a chance, but we can't afford to get it wrong."

"There has to be another way," I say. "If we fire some missiles at their ships, even if they miss, the aliens will at least know about us. Know we're here. If others know besides just those in the company, maybe the settlement will be stopped."

"And what if they don't care?" Colonel Hamilton says. "We can't take that chance. I've made my decision. We will carry out our mission tonight. We leave at oh-one-hundred."

Then he dismisses us.

48

Catlin is really upset. "We can't do this," she says once we're outside the colonel's tent. "We can't let him do this."

Sam says, "I don't like this any more than you, but think about two things: One, he's given an order. If we don't follow it, there are going to be serious consequences. Two, what if this is our only chance to defeat the aliens? It looked impossible before. This is a way to do it. This is a way to save humankind. Maybe this is the third way Running Bird was talking about."

"But—" Catlin says.

"No buts. We have our orders." Sam says she's going to get some rest before we go and we should do the same.

"You don't really believe that, do you?" Catlin asks me. "This can't be the third way. The price is too high."

We go back to our tents. We talk it over. What about drinking water and food supplies and people close to those cities? And fallout? And what if it isn't just a nuclear fall but a nuclear winter?

There are too many what-ifs.

But there's one big what-if in favor of acting. What if we do nothing? What if all those new settlers land?

If they land, there is no what-if. It will all be decided.

49

We leave at exactly one o'clock. It's dark and cool, and the stars fill the sky. There are thirty of us. We take a jeep and three trucks down the mountain, a caravan, with lights on. Catlin and I ride with Captain Wilkes in the jeep. Sam and Michael are farther back, in one of the big trucks loaded with armed soldiers. Somehow Sam managed to convince the colonel to let Michael come. I can't decide if I'm glad to have him along for what might be our final mission or if I'd rather he stayed back at the camp, where he might be safer.

Captain Wilkes orders Catlin and me to weave a cloak around the caravan, and so we do. The captain is impressed, though I can feel him trying not to show it.

We get to the site, which looks like a storage unit for army trucks and jeeps.

"Doesn't look like much of a facility," I say.

"That's the idea," the captain says.

We gather in front of a chain-link fence. The colonel orders some men to use the wire cutters.

"Their security wall is about three feet inside the fence," he says.

We squeeze through the opening in the fence and get to the wall. It's high and thick. It looks a lot like the one at Lord Vertenomous's, but it might be even stronger. I can feel that more than one alien made it.

This is a really bad time for me to travel to another moment, but I do. It's the world turned gray, ash floating everywhere. We live here, at the missile facility, Catlin and Michael and me. Others live here with us, but not many. We live here because it's easier to defend ourselves. Outside, the world is poisoned. The water isn't drinkable and there isn't much food and people are killing each other for what little there is. A lot of people want what we have, our supplies. They're constantly trying to breach our security. We've killed many of them, and many of our own have died, too.

The aliens are gone. I feel that. But the world is dark. It's so dark that it's always night. Fierce winds whip at us from all sides when we step out of one of the buildings. And it's cold, so cold I can't remember what it's like to be warm.

· · • • · ·

"Jesse?" Catlin says.

I'm back in the present moment, standing in front of the wall. Catlin looks worried. "Is everything okay?"

I nod, even though it's a lie. Everything is most definitely not okay. Because I know—*I know*—that the future I just saw, the future with the nuclear fall, is not the future that leads to me and Catlin and Cat in our cozy home. The nuclear winter doesn't clear up after a few years. That world stays dark.

But I still don't know how to stop it. I try again to trace my steps back from the future with Catlin and Cat, but that future feels like a dream. I see us there; I don't see the way back to here.

"Colonel Hamilton," I say, "this won't work. The nuclear fall won't work."

Everyone stares at me. The colonel's expression hardens. "What's this now?"

"I saw it. Just now. I saw a glimpse of the future."

"Seeing the future is not a talent, son. And this is not the time for this discussion."

"I saw that we make nuclear winter."

"You couldn't see," Colonel Hamilton says. "Your nerves are getting to you."

"Were there aliens?" Captain Wilkes says.

Colonel Hamilton glares at him.

"No," I admit. "The aliens weren't there."

Captain Wilkes looks at Colonel Hamilton. "Sorry, sir, but we in the House of Minerva believe the Warrior Spirit has the sight. But I'm satisfied. I'd take winter over the aliens any day."

"That's enough!" Colonel Hamilton snaps. "I don't believe the boy can see the future. And I certainly don't believe he's the Warrior Spirit! But it doesn't matter. We've got a mission to accomplish, and by the gods we'll accomplish it." He swings his rifle toward Catlin and me and tells us to break the wall *now*.

I want to argue some more, to make him see that there has to be another option, but I know it won't do any good. Catlin and I join. The wall isn't weak, but I see how to get through it, and I can tell that Catlin does, too. It takes us five minutes to crack it, and once we do, it's easy to punch a hole. There's no denying that our power together has increased.

The colonel sends his scouts through the hole in the wall to check out the compound. They mindspeak their reports, which I pretend not to hear: There is a small number of aliens in a barracks at the other end of the compound. Apart from that, the place is deserted.

Colonel Hamilton leads the way across the grounds and past several offices and barracks. Suddenly I sense two alien soldiers nearby; they're sleeping in the plane hangar, which is probably how the scouts missed them.

They must sense us, too, because they wake up in time to raise an alarm but not in time to fight. I kill one of them, and Sam, Michael, and five of the colonel's soldiers manage to kill the other. None of us are killed or even wounded.

Captain Wilkes says, "So it's true. You can kill like they kill. It's a hell of a talent."

I can feel the colonel's disapproval even as he's thinking how glad he is that we killed the aliens so quickly. He's thinking I'm more danger than asset and once this mission is over he's going to rethink his decision about me. I'm tempted to tell him the feeling's mutual, but I keep quiet.

We follow the colonel to an office in the plane hangar. The office hides a second room behind it, this one with a steel door and a retina scanner. A computer takes a scan of the colonel's retina before a panel pops out with a keyboard. The door slides open after he enters a code. Then he uses a key for the elevator.

"We go down in two groups," Colonel Hamilton says. "Captain Wilkes, you stay here with your men and guard the doors. Jesse, Catlin, Sam, and Sam's friend— you hold back and come down with the second group."

The first group is all soldiers, plus Captain Sanderson and a sergeant whose name I forget. The colonel disappears through the doors with the first group.

This is wrong, I mindspeak to Sam.

Shut up, she says.

Catlin is right. Destroying the world to save it—to save us—is wrong.

Not destroy. Wound, Sam mindspeaks.

It's going to be worse than Colonel Hamilton thinks. I've seen it.

We have no choice. She is getting frustrated with me. She is a soldier following orders. You don't question orders.

We do have a choice. I've seen a future where the world has not been wounded. It's our world, our beautiful, green, healthy world, and the aliens are gone. It has to be a future where we didn't fire the missiles.

And I think back to the man at the circus who might or might not have been a man, and his saying I'd make a choice to begin or end all choices, and I know this must be the choice. It must be here.

And if you're wrong? Sam's question stabs at me.

Just then the elevator door opens and one of Colonel Hamilton's soldiers motions us to the elevator. We can hear aliens running in their totally uncoordinated way toward the hangar. Captain Wilkes and a couple of his men prepare to hold them off for as long as they can, which I'm afraid won't be very long.

"They run like girls," Michael says.

"This girl could outrun you," Sam says. "And if I can't, I know I can outfight you, so just cut the sexist crap."

"Sorry," he says.

Sam turns to me. "This vision you had, the one where the earth isn't destroyed? You didn't happen to see what we did to get us there, did you?"

"It's not really a vision. It's more like walking ahead in time. Except I don't actually walk. And it's not actually ahead."

"Gods," she mutters. "The Warrior must have been really hard up when he chose you. Can you tell us what we're supposed to do next or not?"

The elevator drops. It goes down fast and far.

"I'll have to show you."

This is a big lie, of course. But I'm desperate, and this at least buys me time.

The elevator door opens again. This time it opens to a large room filled with computer stations. Off to one side is a screen that takes up most of one wall. Auditorium seats are in front of it.

It's the room I saw in one of my travels to the future, which is now the present—the one in which I put Colonel Hamilton in a choke hold, the one where he says I've destroyed us all. What if he's right and I destroy everything? What if I make the wrong choice and end all choices?

Colonel Hamilton is at a computer station. He's typing in codes. The large screen on the wall flashes, and we see a room of missiles. They're white with gray metal tops. They look tall.

We hear gunfire above us: Captain Wilkes and his men guarding the doors. Colonel Hamilton barely registers the noise. He just orders a few soldiers to guard the elevator door.

"I have to reset the destination codes," the colonel says. "I need you two to cloak what I'm doing. The aliens are trying to override my commands from upstairs." His brow is dotted with sweat, the only sign of his struggles. The sound of the elevator going up the shaft startles us all. I realize that the gunfire stopped a while ago.

"Looks like we'll have company soon," Sam says.

The soldiers by the door get into position. I use the distraction to mindspeak to Catlin, to tell her that she needs to read the colonel. We need those codes.

She can't know what I have in mind—I'm not even sure yet myself—but she doesn't hesitate. I feel her pushing into him. The colonel's hands move up and down the keyboard almost like he's playing it. He's very focused. He doesn't notice the soldiers crouching and raising their guns. And he doesn't notice Catlin reading him.

Catlin sends me a message telling me she thinks she has the codes to reset destinations.

Think?

It's not a science.

"Keep those things back for three minutes," Colonel Hamilton orders over his shoulder, "and we'll teach those green devils a thing or two."

A part of me is with him. A part of me thinks he's right. Nuclear fall, nuclear winter, we have to get rid of the aliens. But it's the wrong future. If I know anything, I know that. I choose.

Catlin mindspeaks, *I have faith in you, Jesse.*

I show everyone the world I saw, the future that the bombs will create. Nuclear winter. A dead planet and a dying human race. A slow and painful and sad ending to life on Earth.

"We can't do this," I say.

"Shoot him!" the colonel orders.

The soldiers look from the colonel to me and back again. But no one shoots.

"There's another way," I say. "We attack who we should be attacking. We attack the aliens."

"This is not up for debate!" The colonel shouts. He turns back to his keyboard. "Shoot the girl," he says.

The guns swing toward Catlin, and that's when I do it: I launch myself at Colonel Hamilton, pull him out of his chair, and put him in a choke hold. It's a good one. It's like what I saw when I traveled to this future that is quickly becoming the past.

Some of the guns swing back toward me. The colonel can't speak, but he can mindspeak.

Shoot her! he orders. I put his mind in a choke hold.

All the guns swing toward Catlin again, but still no one shoots. No one wants to be the first to do it.

Sam and Michael take advantage of their hesitation to swing their rifles toward the colonel, whose face is beet red.

"Anyone shoots, a lot of people are going to die," Sam says. "Starting with the colonel."

The soldiers are confused. Some of the rifles swing toward Sam and Michael, but no one fires.

"I have the Spirit of the Warrior in me," I say. "I'm doing what has to be done. That's all I'm doing. I'm doing what has to be done."

Total crap? Truth? Don't know. Don't care at that point. I just need them to remain confused enough to hesitate.

The elevator starts back down.

"Guns toward the door, soldiers," Sam orders.

"Guns toward the door," I echo.

And the soldiers spin around. They point their guns toward the elevator.

I join with Catlin. She can see my plan more easily that way than if I tried to mindspeak it. Quickly she changes the destinations of the missiles. She looks at me and holds my gaze for one long second before she pushes the button to launch the missiles.

The ground shudders, and we can feel them launch. The screen on the wall shows them flying out of the ground and toward the vastness of space. Thirty-six of them. Our last hope.

The colonel goes limp in my arms. I lower him to the ground and take his gun from his holster.

The elevator door opens at the same moment, and guns fire. The aliens stop the bullets. Rifles fly out of some soldiers' hands. I send wave after wave of energy at them to block their attacks and give our men and women a chance to recover, to fight back.

Behind us on the big screen, the missiles make their way toward the ships out in space. Thirty-six missiles on their way. Thirty-six little flashes of light. They're there, and then they aren't. In a second, every missile disappears. Thirty-six dots of light, like candles on a birthday cake, blown out in one frickin' breath.

"You've destroyed us," the colonel chokes out from the floor, his eyes glued to the screen. "You've signed our death warrant."

I turn to Catlin, but she doesn't even see me. She just keeps looking at the screen like she's trying to will the missiles back on. But she can't. We've made our choices. This is where they've led us.

(((((50)))))

Then something none of us expects happens. The aliens stop fighting. The Sanginians put a shield up around themselves for protection, but they don't attack. Sam orders the soldiers to cease fire. Most of them don't have guns to fire anymore anyway. I think these aliens were more prepared for the guns. I think the aliens have been sharing notes on our attacks, which surprises me. These aren't hunters. They're soldiers.

Stand by for a message, we hear from the alien who seems to be in charge.

The last time I heard this was when the aliens invaded and we were made slaves.

PLEASE DO NOT FIRE ANY MORE MISSILES AT US OR WE WILL BE FORCED TO DESTROY YOU. WE MUST PROCESS NEW

INFORMATION. YOUR STATUS IS BEING REVIEWED. WE WILL HAVE AN ANSWER FOR YOU SHORTLY.

The aliens back into the elevator and leave.

Catlin, Michael, Sam, and I are put under arrest. We're taken back to camp. Later that same morning there's a second message.

WE ARE LEAVING NOW. WE HAVE CONCLUDED THAT THE COMPANY MADE MISCALCULATIONS AND MISREPRESENTA-TIONS ABOUT YOUR PLANET, WHICH LED TO AN ILLEGAL SETTLEMENT. A FULL INQUIRY IS IN PROGRESS. HOWEVER, IT IS CLEAR THAT THE SETTLEMENT OF YOUR PLANET WAS A VIOLATION OF SANGINIAN POLICY. THEREFORE, A FULL REFUND WILL BE GIVEN TO EVERY SANGINIAN SETTLER.

WE HEREBY RETURN YOUR PLANET TO YOU, EARTHLINGS. WE DO SO WITH PROFOUND APOLOGIES. WE ARE VERY SORRY FOR YOUR LOSSES.

ALL SURVIVORS, MOSTLY THE YOUNG ONES OF YOUR SPECIES, TAKEN BY US WILL BE RETURNED TO YOUR PLANET, THOUGH THIS MAY REQUIRE A FEW OF YOUR MONTHS TO ACCOMPLISH AS THEY HAVE BEEN SENT TO TRAINING STATIONS. WE WISH YOU A FORTUNATE FUTURE.

SINCERELY,
SANGINIAN SECRETARY OF SETTLEMENT, LORD HADRIAN

EPILOGUE

They leave. It takes them a little longer to leave than it took them to invade. But they're gone in twenty days. By my calendar, the last alien leaves August 1. In the future, August 1 will be celebrated as the day the earth became ours again. And it is ours, but who we are has changed. The survivors all have talents. That's one big change. But something that hasn't changed is humankind's desire for power. There are gangs and even, already, small armies led by men and women who make all kinds of claims for a future in which they lead. The government of old America is fragmented and slow to reform. It gives these armies a chance to get recruits and territory. One of them is said to be led by a powerful and charismatic young man who claims he is destined to unite the talented.

Catlin and I have been asked to leave Colonel Hamilton's camp. He wants us out of his sight. He's still saying that if he had his way, we'd be before a firing squad, but he won't have his way. We're heroes to many.

Most of the members of New America, as well as a few people from Colonel Hamilton's unit, want to leave with us when I say we plan to make the dangerous trip to Austin, Texas, where the new government of

Texas is rumored to be forming. They want me to lead them there. There are many rebel gangs between us and Austin, but, as far as we know, there are none of the more dangerous armies that range to the north and particularly to the east of us.

Some of the members of New America choose to stay at the military camp, though. Sam and Michael are among them.

It's Sam who wants to stay. She says New America will need soldiers and Colonel Hamilton, whatever weakness of character he might have, will be loyal to the government. She will be needed. She wants to fight. Michael is in love, and he says he wants to fight for New America, too.

"I owe you everything," he tells me. "But I want to fight, too. And I'm whipped, bro. Let's face it."

Sam rolls her eyes, but I can feel that she feels something strong for him, too.

I tell him I'll see him soon.

We both know that isn't likely.

I lead trips into surrounding towns to get vehicles and supplies. We make several trips into Albuquerque to get things we need. Finally, one dawn, we're ready to go and we say our good-byes and we're off. We hope at the end of this trip to find a new beginning. I guess this is another way we haven't changed. Some of our ancestors, long ago, came to America driven by the same hope, looking for the same new beginning. They called it the New World then. It's our new world now.

THE THE END